PRAISE FOR JOSH EMMONS

A MORAL TALE AND OTHER MORAL TALES

"This is one of the best books I've read in ages—a whip-smart and painfully lucid collection of stories, full of haunting observations and astonishing sentences. Over and over again, these stories ask what it means to make a moral judgment, without ever making that judgment for us; they resist easy explanations and obvious resolutions, and leave us in a raw and reawakened state of human clarity."

—Jess Row, author of *Your Face in Mine*

"I enjoyed and admired every page of *A Moral Tale*. Josh Emmons has written an exquisitely strange and deeply intelligent suite of stories about love and desire, how we pursue, deny, and are ultimately— whether we like it or not—defined by b(

—Vu Tran, author of *Dragonfish*

THE LOSS OF LEON MEED

"Emmons writes with crisp, gratifying authority. As Leon Meed pops up peculiarly, he takes excellent advantage of his character's mobility.... *The Loss of Leon Meed* has considerable appeal...and succeeds in finding comic potential in unlikely places. Its developments are jauntily clever...and the novel has a well-developed screwball quality that keeps it buoyant. Emmons has characters bumping into one another unawares until they form a web of interconnection. [He] is wise."

—*The New York Times*

"An audaciously ambitious first novel...[not] merely determined to dazzle with weirdness. *The Loss of Leon Meed* is a canny status report on the American soul...engaging, enigmatic."

—*The Los Angeles Times*

"Here's how you know Josh Emmons is the real deal: he's created a full spectrum of Californian characters who are ludicrous and ill-behaved and lovable in equal measure; he's a major-league prose writer who has fun in every sentence without ever showing off or hitting a phony note; and you want to keep reading him for the pure pleasure of his company."

—Jonathan Franzen, author of *Freedom* and *The Corrections*

"A madcap parable about an unwitting Houdini named Leon Meed... [which] leaves us hungry for more. Emmons cycles through and illuminates the plights of his diverse, crowded cast—including a recovering alcoholic, an overweight therapist, and a Korean hippie—with a finesse that approaches that of a seasoned literary ventriloquist. The characters' stories take on a cumulative, mesmerizing rhythm."

—*The New York Times Book Review*

"As remarkable and moving a portrait of America as I have seen in some time. Josh Emmons pieces together the emotional life of a small city with a wit and range that recalls Robert Altman's Nashville. Mature yet playful, fanciful yet brimming with the details of contemporary life, *The Loss of Leon Meed* leaves us with an odd feeling of hard-won hope. The hope that in our society kindness and reason may one day prevail."

—Gary Shteyngart, author of *Super Sad True Love Story*

"From the most unlikely of circumstances—a man who has come unstuck in time—Emmons constructs a story that is both wholly original and poignantly familiar. Part mystery, part meditation on longing, part love story, *The Loss of Leon Meed* is a gripping, evocative, heart-wrenching novel."

—Alison Smith, author of *Name All the Animals*

"In an imaginative and eminently readable debut, Emmons binds together a roster of strangers in a weirdly likable tale of the supernatural. In a very fanciful way, [he] lovingly carves very believable people out of the mists of California and displays them amidst the cacophony of their lives. A witty and sparkling debut."

—*Kirkus Reviews* (starred review)

"A promising debut."

—*Publishers Weekly*

"Emmons's imaginative debut novel [is threaded] with interesting meditations on religion, psychotherapy, death, and fate. [He] shows considerable flair in his striking ability to give his whimsical premise such philosophical overtones."

—*Booklist*

"Emmons dazzles with his sentences, taking risks with all the writerly challenges...and nailing each like a young Jonathan Franzen."

—*SF Weekly*

"This wise and lovely book both understands the troubles of these times and soothes them."

—*New Orleans Times-Picayune*

"What a pleasure to be welcomed to a brand-new world. Josh Emmons's Eureka, mapped with well-chosen details and a sympathetic eye, is populated by terrific characters whose quests for love, faith, and mystery interlock with delicate grace and humor. I enjoyed them all, especially the enigmatic Leon Meed. His loss is our gain."

—Glen David Gold, author of *Carter Beats the Devil*

"Witty, compassionate, and imaginatively structured, Josh Emmons's debut is one of those novels that make you think, 'Only in California.'"
—Adam Langer, author of *Crossing California*

"Josh Emmons's gorgeous and heartrending novel is imbued with rare intelligence and even rarer compassion. *The Loss of Leon Meed* is like a cathedral, in which our wanton failings and unexpected triumphs are gracefully laid bare, and the ensemble cast is its choir, a concert of perfectly pitched and exquisitely aching voices singing of hope and grief, of being lost and, at last, of being found."
—Bret Anthony Johnston, author of *Remember Me Like This*

PRESCRIPTION FOR A SUPERIOR EXISTENCE

"'The imagination is always at an end of an era.' Frank Kermode quotes this line from Wallace Stevens to highlight the way some of us Western-bred humans tend to impose a structure on time that accords with our own lifetime: here we are, we tell ourselves, at the end of history...Emmons's clever speculative tale takes that old story and sets it against a backdrop of contemporary environmental and political threats, satirizing American-style credulity about the end of time...at times the book resembles something Philip K. Dick might have written had he lived to experience the climate crisis...it is entertaining."
—*The New York Times Book Review*

"If the title of Josh Emmons's sophomore novel, *Prescription for a Superior Existence*, sounds more like a Dr. Phil-type self-help book than a work of fiction, that's entirely purposeful. Emmons takes on trendy religious sects like Scientology and Kabbalah in the story of a thirty-something man disgusted with his life, who turns to a group called the Prescription for a Superior Existence to find a more fulfilling life, or at least a more fulfilling lifestyle, and winds up getting forced into the group's training camp against his will."

—*The Boston Globe*

"In *Prescription for a Superior Existence*, Josh Emmons successfully avoids the second-novel jinx, following up on his bravura debut, *The Loss of Leon Meed*, with a neat little metaphysical thriller that manages to combine satire and seriousness, social commentary and science fiction. It's probably unfair that someone so young should be so talented, but the obvious ambition of Emmons's efforts and the degree of his success on his own terms belies the constant currently fashionable moaning and groaning about the 'death of literacy.'...by the end of this witty, wise novel, he has demonstrated how character and destiny are inextricably intertwined."

—*San Francisco Chronicle*

"Josh Emmons's *Prescription for a Superior Existence*...is erudite and engaging; it is poignant and often moving; it is intelligent and lucid. It makes crafty and craftsman-like use of objects. It is even blessed with an empathetic and vulnerable first-person narrator."

—*Harvard Book Review*

"Emmons has put his finger on the pulse of a bizarre vein in American religious history that has spawned everything from the Shaker religion to Scientology, from the Branch Davidians to the Yearning for Zion Ranch. He demonstrates an understanding of the process of spiritual seduction...with interesting plot twists and hard-won insights."

—*The Seattle Times*

"Readers will be caught up in the narrative, as well as the unusual premise and snarky humor of this offbeat novel."

—*Booklist*

"A novel about an ordinary man and religion—the creepy, California kind."

—*People*

"Emmons rakes a herd of sacred cows over the coals in this unusual novel.... Readers with a penchant for satire and the absurd will relish the novel's outrageous premise and knowing jibes at popular culture's sacred and secular excesses."

—*Library Journal*

"Emmons's yarn is engaging."

—*Publishers Weekly*

"With *Prescription for a Superior Existence*, Josh Emmons has created a wholly original, brave, and disturbingly plausible novel, an existential, theological, fin du monde thriller about star-crossed orphans, twenty-first-century cults, environmental angst, and the extremes and consequences of desire."

—James P. Othmer, author of *The Futurist*

"In *Prescription for a Superior Existence*, Josh Emmons's hero Jack Smith—a man of questionable appetites, high skepticism, and touching vulnerability—falls through the rabbit hole of newfangled California religion. The result is an acidly hilarious, tightly plotted adventure that folds big themes, romantic moments, and a little thing called the end of the world into its pages. Both a wicked skewering of religious cults and a finely wrought testament to their power, this novel reads like Raymond Chandler rollicking through the house of L. Ron Hubbard. It's as probing and smart as it is moving, hopeful, and sweet."

—Alix Ohlin, author of *Babylon and Other Stories*

A MORAL TALE
AND
OTHER MORAL TALES

ALSO BY JOSH EMMONS

The Loss of Leon Meed

Prescription for a Superior Existence

A MORAL TALE

AND OTHER MORAL TALES

STORIES

JOSH EMMONS

DZANC
BOOKS

DZANC BOOKS

5220 Dexter Ann Arbor Rd.
Ann Arbor, MI 48103
www.dzancbooks.org

Library of Congress Cataloging-in-Publication Data

Names: Emmons, Josh, author.
Title: A moral tale : and other moral tales / Josh Emmons.
Description: Ann Arbor, MI : Dzanc Books, 2017.
Identifiers: LCCN 2016031326 | ISBN 9781941088807
Classification: LCC PS3605.M574 A6 2017 | DDC 813/.6--dc23
LC record available at https://lccn.loc.gov/2016031326

First US edition: April 2017
Interior design by Michelle Dotter

This is a work of fiction. Characters and names appearing in this work are a product of the author's imagination, and any similarity to real persons, living or dead, is coincidental and not intended by the author.

Printed in the United States of America

10   9   8   7   6   5   4   3   2   1

CONTENTS

A MORAL TALE
AND OTHER MORAL TALES

A MORAL TALE

The south of France is like the north of France. People fall in and out of love. No one knows how to sauté anything anymore. The revolution left after a noisy round of charades, and late capitalism locked the door behind it. Will China look down? Does Canada matter? The New World wants softer lighting, and the answer is a string of tinsel laid over an open grate. In the north and south of France, cinema is dying and abstract art is dying and videography is dying and sound collage is dying. Stendhal said, "Far less envy in America, and far less wit." Celine said, "Sadness has different ways of getting to people, but it succeeds almost every time." Love isn't fatal and death, like the Gulf Stream, circulates heat. "God's only excuse is that he doesn't exist," continued Stendhal, with the south and north of France already two sides of a coin so faded no one could tell up from down.

Bernard got a job after college at Learn!, a company that made educational software, working on the sequel to a video game in which players used math formulas to beat up trolls and shoot flaming arrows into the hearts of troll villages. In January, he agreed to move in with his cousin Veronique, who lived outside the city center on welfare because of arthritis in her knee, and who smoked marijuana most mornings in a park next to a statue of Charles de Gaulle, whose arms were raised in triumph. The park had backless benches. An old wiry mime in patchy makeup and ripped ballet slippers—and with a slight bulge in his leotard—did a trembling impression of the statue all day. Growing up, Bernard had seen Veronique twice a year at family dinners, when she'd told him about reggae and the divine lion of Rastafarianism. Or was it the divine light? France needed to either outgrow mime or embrace it again. De Gaulle hadn't rescued the country from evil in World War II. That had been the fresh Americans and battered British and endless Russians. Bernard thought reggae sounded like trampolining in one's head, and moved in with Veronique instead of getting a place by himself, as he'd wanted to do, because Veronique's mother, his aunt Janine, had begged him, hoping that his presence would inspire her daughter to go to college or get a job or at least stop sleeping with the deadbeat roommates she kept finding on so-called lifestyle websites.

On Bernard's first night in the apartment, Veronique lit a joint from her breast pocket and said, "Why're you looking at dwarves?"

He opened a window, having lost his asthma inhaler a month before. "What?"

"On your computer, those frightening people."

"They're trolls in the game I'm working on."

"Are they?" She ashed her joint into a Moroccan dipping bowl. "My friend Odette just got divorced—it's freezing in here—and I think you two would get along."

Bernard watched a man on the street peeing into a trash can. "What's this neighborhood like, exactly?"

"I can invite her over right now and put on some calypso, have a dance party." Veronique grabbed a phone, its screen cracked into twin spider webs.

"There's a guy outside—"

She held up a silencing finger and talked into the phone, then set it down and said that Odette was at work at a bakery where her manager was ex-military from America or Alaska or somewhere, the point being he was an asshole, so she couldn't come over but would have them to dinner the next day.

Bernard went to bed and for an hour heard laughter coming from the living room television, then forty minutes of panting, then a long, low-grind blender. He kept flipping his pillow over to get to the cool side. Eventually it became morning and he took a walk on sidewalks slick with black ice and saw that in this part of the city what broke or was abandoned stayed broken and abandoned. The cold made it all throb in place. He passed empty storefronts and Halal butchers and Gypsy kids selling iguanas and a block-long souk with spices like varicolored dunes rippling across linked tables.

At Our Lady of the Immaculate Heart, Bernard heard the slow peal and repeal of a pipe organ coming through wide, ivory-inlaid doors. He drew up his jacket collar and blew on his numb fingers until they tingled with pain. A posted itinerary said that Father Maazi's sermon was about to begin. It would be on mercy.

Inside the cathedral, Bernard sat on a straight-backed pew with worn velvet seat cushions. A dozen old dowagers and middle-aged couples were scattered around, plus a young woman whose blond hair was pulled back by a black barrette. The barrette looked like a sleeping moth. Father Maazi, a tall Senegalese man made triangular by his sacerdotal robes, floated up to the pulpit and gave a benediction in Latin, then led the Lord's Prayer in French. The congregants murmured along with him. During his sermon on mercy, the exercise of which raised man above all other creatures, even angels, whose programmed nature made them incapable of it, Bernard kept glancing over at the blonde. She had long eyelashes, a Roman nose, a thin white scar that ran from her ear to her jaw in a parabolic arc, and the open expression of someone either transported by what she heard or daydreaming. Mercy was the easiest yet most difficult virtue. It cost you nothing but the illusion that your interests were separate from other people's.

After mass he watched the blonde climb onto a step-through bicycle with swept-back handlebars, green streamers, and a bronze bell and tuck in her skirt so it wouldn't flare open in the wind. A minute later, pedaling past him, she slid on a patch of ice and crashed to the ground.

"Are you all right?" he asked, jogging over to her.

"I think so." She got up and righted her twisted bicycle, inspecting a jagged scratch in its frame. "The street is like a skating rink."

He felt pinpricks on his face from snow beginning to fall. "I saw you at church just now, and I wonder if you know anything about its social programs, like if it has an addict support group? I'm looking for someplace to take my cousin who's on drugs."

The woman brushed snowflakes from her bicycle seat, touched the sleeve of her coat to her nose. "This was my first time to visit there. I heard music while riding by before and went in because of that."

Adrenaline surged through him and the woman didn't climb back onto her bicycle. "Are you American?" he asked.

"No."

"Canadian?"

"No."

She was from Wales, an exchange student at the local university. They talked about Swansea and the price of bicycle paint and whether mercy meant sparing someone pain or promoting their happiness— that is, was it passive or active in nature?—and made plans to meet that evening on the other side of the city at a café called the Rumba Room. Her name was Sally. She seemed like a woman who could lose an art contest and just fold her arms in disappointment—feel a compression of the heart, yes, but not go out and get drunk and sleep with a stranger and tell Bernard he shouldn't have been studying when she got the bad news about the contest, so that his neglect rather than her lack of self-control had caused her infidelity, which wasn't in fact a big deal. No, Sally seemed nothing like Claire, his ex-fiancée, who'd said when he ended it, "You don't understand nuance. What's not on the surface is invisible to you. Thank God this is happening."

Odette opened the door of her studio apartment and said, "You're late."

"We had to walk since the buses aren't running." Veronique kissed her friend on both cheeks and unwrapped the icy scarf from around her neck. "The snow's waist-high out there."

"Is that true, Bernard?" Odette said his name slowly, almost sighing the second syllable, and stepped aside so they could enter a narrow room with a kitchenette along one wall, two apple-green bean bags in the middle, and stacks of boxes in the far corner, like a distant metropolis, beside a large mattress covered in tangled sheets. "Throw your coats on the rug. I've got wine, brandy, or coffee."

Veronique said wine and Bernard coffee as they peeled off layers and picked at frozen knots in their shoelaces.

"Ignore the boxes. Hans won't let me keep anything in our old apartment because he's teaching me a lesson." Odette, in a striped apron and with jet-black hair swelling into a low-wave pompadour, handed them paper cups. "I heard you almost got married, Bernard."

Veronique tossed back her wine and picked through a pile of clothes on the floor. "Can I borrow this?" she asked, holding up a loose-knit wool sweater.

"If you give back my suede boots. There's a relief, don't you think, Bernard, when you hit bottom in a relationship. After falling for so long and all that anticipation, the impact isn't so bad."

He said, "Mine happened suddenly."

"Are you sure I still have those boots?" Veronique asked. "Because I remember giving them back."

"You don't remember anything," said Odette.

When it had become clear that Bernard and Veronique would have to walk two miles through the snow to reach Odette's apartment, he'd tried to get out of it, but Veronique said they should spend time together because they hardly knew each other, and Odette had already made them pastries, and walking was good exercise, and he owed her for what she'd done for him. *What've you done for me?* he asked, as she pinched out a joint and told him to forget it, her eyelids heavy like an iguana's.

Odette whisked a thin yellow liquid in a bowl.

"If we're not eating yet," said Veronique, "let's put on music and do some dancing."

Bernard's legs ached and he looked at Odette, who said, "I have to finish the glaze."

"Where're your speakers? I can set them up at an angle to get the best acoustics for this space." Veronique put her ear against a wall and knocked on it, as if listening for mice.

Bernard said to her, "I'm surprised you're able to dance."

She frowned and went to the kitchenette and refilled her wine cup and looked at him blankly.

"Because of the arthritis in your knee," he said.

"Knees. Listen, I meant to tell you before, but if the Disabilities Services Department calls and asks about it, about my arthritis, say you don't know anything because I never discuss it because it depresses me."

His coffee tasted like wood smoke. "Why would they call and ask that?"

"It's something they do."

"You want me to lie to them?"

"It's not lying, since we haven't discussed it."

"We're discussing it now."

"No, we're discussing whether we've discussed it." Veronique's cheeks were turning pink or maybe auburn, and her dreadlocks formed a Medusan squall on her head. She finished the wine and poured more. "This is serious. My livelihood is at stake."

"But if you're okay and get disability checks, that's fraud."

Above the metallic whir of her fork against the bowl, Odette said, "You guys should relax on the bean bags for a minute. My friend gave them to me who never used them."

Veronique said, "How do you figure fraud?"

"Because you're taking money under false pretenses from the government," said Bernard.

"A rent subsidy and food vouchers?"

"If enough people did the same thing, it'd bankrupt the country. You should get a job. Then you wouldn't have to worry about getting found out."

She stepped toward him, her face a mixture of confusion and anger and fear and incredulity and guilt and scorn, then shook her head, turned around, and picked up her coat from the rug. "I told my mother I'd take you in since you're having a hard time." Struggling to put on waterlogged shoes. "But this isn't working out. You can stay another few days, till the weekend, but after that find someplace else to live." Yanking open the front door, she said, "And don't touch the phone."

Odette looked up from her bowl. "What're you doing?"

"Those boots were in the sack of things I returned before the roots festival in October, when I gave you the skeleton lamp."

"No, they weren't, and I didn't want that lamp. Come have an olive."

Veronique slammed the door behind her.

———

Outside falling snow hid parked cars and trees and rooftops, haloed street lamps, softened the atmosphere. Bernard and Odette sat at a small round table eating pastries filled with curried potatoes, raisins, carrots, lentils, and persimmons. She asked him why he'd studied math. He said it was because his father had been a mathematician. Also, Galileo had called math the language God used to write the universe. Odette said she'd enjoyed doing linear equations in school because they were like recipes, a set of unique ingredients fusing into something whole. Bernard excused himself to go to the bathroom, where he splashed cold water on his face. He should've left after Veronique did and gone to wait at the Rumba Room for Sally. It was nine thirty. He found a porn magazine in a stack of cooking journals leaning against the bathtub. A page was ripped out.

Back at the table, he didn't touch his coffee. Odette had removed her apron and wore a V-neck blouse over a mauve chemisette. She looked somewhere between thirty and forty years old. By calling math the language with which God wrote the universe, Bernard said, Galileo had suggested that all three phenomena—language, God, and the universe—were discreet but interconnected mysteries. An overlapping trinity of infinities. Bernard undid the top two buttons of his shirt and wiped his forehead and said that you could no sooner read the last imaginable sentence than you could find the edge of God or reach the end of the universe.

Odette chewed for a long time. "But the universe is expanding," she finally said. "So it doesn't go on forever and you could get to the end of it with a fast enough spaceship."

The picture of Sally in Bernard's mind had turned into a faint, semi-translucent image, like a daytime moon. On his plate was a bed of golden flakes. "There can never be a fast enough spaceship," he said.

Odette leaned back in her chair. The radio played an old Breton folk song with a Caribbean arrangement. Her eyebrows were as thin as bird wings on the horizon. She said, "You should eat the last pastry."

"Thanks, but I have to go in a minute. I'm meeting a friend at ten."

"Oh?" She got up and cleared the plates and set them on the kitchen counter noiselessly. Her dress hung to her calves, a delicate brown. "Then take my umbrella. It's in one of the boxes, I think."

The green bean bags in the middle of the room were shiny and shaped like dewdrops. A dark wet ring surrounded Bernard's shoes on the rug. Last summer he had applied to a PhD program and proposed working on the problem that had occupied his father at the end of his life, Goldbach's conjecture, a proof that all even integers greater than 2 could be expressed as the sum of two primes. His rejection from the university came just after Claire announced she was engaged to someone else. On the phone, Aunt Janine told him to calm down, to breathe, but how could he breathe calmly when he was supposed to carry on his father's work, and Claire was supposed to ask him to forgive her? Aunt Janine said he could apply again next year, and Claire was an idiot. Also, Veronique's roommate had just moved out. The third one that year. Veronique, she said, was twenty-eight and adrift in the world. Bernard wondered what that had to do with anything. Aunt Janine said, *You've got to help her. I've done all I can do.*

"I'm sorry about earlier," he said. "What happened with Veronique."

Odette ran the faucet and put on a pair of yellow latex gloves, the rubbery snap of each fitted finger sounding like tiny whip cracks. "She shouldn't have asked you to lie."

"Thanks for saying so, because—"

"But you shouldn't have refused."

He watched her slide the dishes under a white stream of water, heard a hiss and submarine clanking. "Veronique can't sit around all day getting high," he said.

"Why not?"

"She needs a job." He tried to think of a reason. "To give her life meaning."

"Most people hate their jobs." Odette stacked the plates and then scrubbed a cherrywood cutting board. "You're going to be late for your friend."

He looked at his phone. "They texted and said they can't make it. Because the snow's getting worse out there."

Glancing over her shoulder: "Is that true, Bernard?"

He swallowed. "Yes."

Steam rose from the silver sink like censer smoke. "Then you'll have to stay the night."

Odette gave him a new toothbrush with rubber stripes along its sides. For better grip. He went into the bathroom, and although the porn magazine was still there, he studied a pyramid of hand soaps on the shelf above the toilet. Each of its four corners was a different shade of yellow. When he came out, she had changed into a sleeveless nightgown and lay on the mattress with a blanket folded back at her waist. Her hair, let down and parted in the middle, crashed gently onto the pillow behind her. A candle on the windowsill gave the room its only light. Bernard pushed the two bean bags together and got into a horizontal position.

"Are you comfortable on those?" she asked.

He nodded. "I love bean bags."

Odette's body took up barely a third of the mattress. "Nobody loves bean bags," she said.

He felt the beans squeeze tightly together as he shifted his body. "You must like your job, since you make pastries in your free time. I know a masseuse and she never gives her boyfriend massages."

"You want to talk about work?"

"Veronique said your boss is mean."

Odette placed her palms flat on the mattress and gave him an incredulous smile, like he'd broken in to rob her and then called the police. "He's a Francophile, so everything we make is classically French: éclairs and friands and gougéres. It's boring. He lost a foot in Iraq, and the hospital served him Freedom Fries. Let's talk about something else."

Bernard's fingers stuck to the vinyl surface of the lower bean bag. "How did you meet Veronique?"

"Hans used to play in a reggae band she liked, Natty Dresden, and he'd come to all of their shows."

Bernard's mother had left France when he was fifteen to live with someone she'd met in San Francisco. His father took him to a steakhouse soon afterward and got drunk and told him they'd be fine without her. No, they'd be great, because now they could do all the father/son things they hadn't been able to do before: eat frozen food, go to weeknight football games, watch action movies, visit strip clubs. Bernard would have been embarrassed by these plans, but his thoughts were full of friends and school and girls and music, and he paid no attention to them. When his father got lymphoma a year later, he said, *You shouldn't have smoked when you were young*, and found excuses not to escort him home from the treatment center. *Can't you call a cab or get Aunt Janine to take you?*

Odette said, "I wish I had an extra blanket for you. You're going to get cold."

"I never get cold."

"That's lucky. I'm always cold."

Bernard could barely keep his eyes open. "Why don't you get a space heater?"

"They're fire hazards." She rubbed her arms and her nightgown didn't slip down her shoulders. She didn't sigh or propose that they work on linear equations or say, *Bernard, I'm going to tell you something you already know but won't admit, although if you did then a lot of what's wrong here, like your lying on those stupid bean bags when I'm cold and alone on a huge mattress, and your having invented that text from your friend, and your unmerciful speech to Veronique about fraud, might be fixed: your aunt didn't ask you to move in with your cousin because she thought you could save her. On the contrary.*

After a minute, he got up from the bean bags and lay down next to Odette. His clothes were uncomfortable at first, but then they weren't. She blew out the candle and breathed evenly. With his legs he explored the empty space at the bottom of the mattress. As he adjusted to the darkness and Odette came into view as gradations of black, along with the room's furniture and boxes and clothes, he saw, without surprise, with a kind of relief, that what lay beneath the surface was just a darker version of what lay above.

The north and south of France are full of people who by acting in plain sight will never be caught. They live in the Old World, which is newer than the Ancient World. Stendhal worshipped Emperor Napoleon and Celine embraced fascism. When known as Gaul, France was occupied by barbarians whose ancestors had drawn bison on cave walls. These drawings broke down motion into its constituent parts. Napoleon's dream of a unified Europe survived him, and fascism was the idea of order worked out to the nth degree. Does this explain the later popularity of surrealism or *musique concrete* or New Wave cinema or the Pompidou Centre or Jacques Chirac, who as Minister of Culture forbade Americanisms like "les blue jeans" and "le weekend" from being spoken on the radio? To be French is to be heir to Indo-china and Algeria, as well as to secularism and accordion love songs designed to drown out infidelity and cancer and regret. Trolls must be burned alive. If you show them mercy, they'll destroy you. It's their nature.

Bernard couldn't see the sun when he left Odette's apartment building in the morning, but it seemed to light the world from within. The snow on the ground was blinding. He turned toward Veronique's apartment and Odette had said to him, *Goodbye, Bernard. It was a pleasure meeting you.*

After cutting through an indoor shopping arcade and crossing two parking lots, he entered Liberation Park, where a flock of elderly Chinese women in baggy pants and sweatshirts swiveled in unison, carving out shapes in the air. Beside a statue of Charles de Gaulle, an old Frenchman in uneven pancake makeup embraced the sky.

"Hey!"

Bernard turned around and saw Veronique sitting a few feet away on a bench, headphones in her lap and a burning joint in her right hand. She smiled and said, "I told you, you and Odette would get along, and here it is the next morning."

He said, "I'll call friends today to ask if I can stay with them while I find a new place."

She took a long drag and patted the bench beside her. "Sit down. You don't have to move out. I was drunk last night. Alcohol affects me badly."

"I shouldn't have accused you of fraud."

"Why not?" Taking another drag. "It's fraud."

They sat in silence for a minute.

"Can I have some of that?" he said, indicating the joint.

"Thought you had asthma."

"One hit won't hurt."

His phone buzzed, a number he didn't recognize. He held it to his ear, and a woman's voice said, "Bernard? Hello, it's Sally from yesterday. I'm sorry for not meeting you at the café, but it was snowing so bad and I lost my phone. My friend called the Rumba Room for me, but no one answered. And now I found my phone. Maybe you'd like to meet for coffee, if you're free?"

"I'm with my cousin right now."

"The cousin on drugs?"

He exhaled a stream of invisible smoke. "We're watching a mime."

"Does he pretend to be trapped inside a box?"

"This one doesn't do that. You should come see him."

He gave Sally directions to the park, then got up and dropped money into the empty cap lying at the mime's feet. Veronique clapped. The mime wasn't trembling. Bernard said to him, "Don't go anywhere." The mime gazed steadily into the distance. Bernard turned to look in that direction, at an expanse of white that seemed to have no beginning and no end. It was beautiful and hostile. Veronique continued to clap and a light breeze started up from the west.

NU

The stream behind Alice's house fed into a river that led to the ocean. Besides men and women out hiking, and children skipping school, she sometimes saw deer, birds, and stray cats along its banks. She was afraid of cats, which had been gods to the ancient Egyptians, a death-struck people. The section of stream that divided her property ran down current from Mandrake Woods, a large forest that covered a sea of natural gas. This sea was either confined and in need of release or contained and best left alone. Whether it was confined or contained depended on whether humans had as many rights as they had obligations in the human era, the Anthropocene, now underway.

The week before, a man named Carl had come to Alice's house and told her about a town hall meeting to discuss gas drilling at Mandrake. A company had made a bid on the land. If she valued the stream, he said, she had to protest the drilling, because it would poison Mandrake's substrata and kill off fish, algae, amphibians, birds, and other creatures that used its waterways. Carl had bad posture but strong, cloudless teeth. In his left hand he held an impact report drawn up by biologists who took no money from energy companies and cared only for science. He wore blue canvas sneakers with a slight elevation at the heel.

After Carl left, a woman stopped by and said that the company asking to drill beneath Mandrake Woods would in fact use safe, ecologically sound methods, and that it would restore the area to its original condition afterward. If anything, the water and wildlife would be in better shape. This woman had been a year ahead of Alice in high school. Her name was Didi then but now it was Celeste, and her long, blond hair had been dyed red and shaped into a playful bob with curls framing her ears. More to the point: natural gas emitted thirty percent less carbon dioxide than oil, a statistic the impact report failed to mention. With the world's energy needs growing daily, the report's authors were foolishly advising that the perfect be the enemy of the good.

Alice's father had started building this house before she was born, but it was still unfinished when she left for college, so she'd grown up in a leafy neighborhood in the nearby town of Kent. She'd returned to live in this remote house for the first time four months ago, upon the suspension of her marriage. There were unwired rooms and unhung doors. The paint was flaky, the sump tank cracked, and the chimney a ziggurat home to squirrels and bats. Otherwise it was in good condition. Her mother, who also hated cats, being allergic to them (or allergic to the glycoprotein in cat saliva), had suggested that she water the dirt path beside the stream so that people would find it muddy and quit using it. Privacy was important for a woman living alone.

Alice's husband, Marouf, would have thought watering the path a terrible idea and worried about someone breaking their ankle—or worse. Hikers were generally unprepared for the procession from one world into the next, unlike the ancient Egyptians, who—from closely studying death and revering cats—had learned a great deal about the Underworld, which they called *Duat*.

As a girl, Alice had played hide-and-seek in Mandrake Woods and knew all of its secret spots. One day she went home after a game and found her mother wiping slurred mascara from her eyes. "Your father," her mother said, "isn't a bad man. We need to remember that."

The suspension of Alice's marriage had happened suddenly. One day she and Marouf were spicing lamb cubes and making potato salad together, and the next she was packing her bags to drive 125 miles back to the unfinished house near Kent. According to the ancients, people were a combination of *ka*, spirit, and *ba*, body. For the former to begin its journey through Duat it first had to discard the latter. That was the easy part. Alice took painkillers for her back because years earlier a group of drunken men driving to a bait shop had run a red light and smashed into her car. She'd met Marouf in the hospital, where she was fitted with a lumbar brace and he worked as a registered nurse. He said to her while she waited for a cab beneath the hospital awning, in controlled pain, during a downpour, "I hate rain. It makes me think of mold and decay. Is that weird?" But there was nothing weird about this, for Marouf's ancestors were from Egypt, where the embalming process had been perfected long before by wrapping corpses so tightly that moisture couldn't seep through the linen layers glued fast by liquid resin. She gave him her phone number even though he didn't ask for it.

Kent was not doing well. The decline of the steel industry had created a sinkhole that took many businesses in the area down with it. The literature Celeste left with Alice promised that natural gas drilling would bring back the town's financial health. In addition to creating jobs, the company would pay local landowners to run conveyance pipes over their properties, and it would contribute taxes to the county and state. Wealth would ripple out across the calm surface of the community.

Alice's father once said to her mother, "We can't afford to finish the extra rooms, but let's install the well and at least use the part of the house that's already done." Her mother had stood up from the cheap plastic table that filled the kitchen and raised her voice. "As if it's a mystery why we can't afford it! As if it's an accident that the money goes to a college trust fund in a town in North Carolina where you had a conference! I saw the boy's report card that woman sent. You won't need to save much."

When her parents argued, Alice would escape in her mind to an underground cave and float along a shallow river in a wide-bottomed wooden boat where it was silent but for the sound of water dripping from the cave's ceiling, as soothing as a mother's heartbeat.

Carl had told her about the effect on water of the hundred or so chemicals used in hydrofracturing, also called fracking, the process whereby natural gas was removed from the ground. The water became flammable. If you put a lighter beneath a running faucet it would burst into flames, like a chemistry experiment gone wrong. Carl directed her to a series of illustrative videos. That night she took extra painkillers and ate soft crackers in bed while watching clips of water on fire.

Finally she fell asleep and had a dream. The dream was set in a circus tent where Carl hung from a red rope clenched between his teeth, twirling around with his arms akimbo high above a wading pool. In a white cape, his face turned upward, he looked like a whirling dervish ascending. Celeste sat next to Alice in the audience rattling a bag of burnt popcorn, and said, "You know why he's able to do that? Fluoride in the water. Look it up in an almanac if you don't believe me."

Duat resembled the land of the living in that it had mountains, rivers, trees, fields, lakes, variable weather, and islands. Without proper training you might arrive and mistake it for the world you'd left behind, and then be surprised by its insect-headed giants and flying, blade-tipped wheels. Your goal in Duat was to overcome these and other obstacles in order to reach Anubis, the god who would hold up your heart with a feather to see if its good outweighed its bad. On the basis of this you would either pass on to eternal paradise or slip back into *Nu*, the primordial waters from which all matter originally came. If you made it to paradise you (or your *ka*) would be reunited with your body and join the gods, including many cats. But if you went to Nu, your *ka* would dissolve into its surroundings never to be reconstituted, like a cup of water placed in the ocean.

Marouf, who after four months of marital suspension still did not fathom the why of it, had called Alice every week. If she answered she'd tell him about which animals and people had come to the stream that morning. She'd describe the markings on this deer or the dirty mouth on that boy. At last he said that if he'd done something to upset her, she should tell him. People had a right to know what they were being accused of. She said it wasn't that simple. His actions— everyone's actions—couldn't be weighed properly in this world, because weight was relative here. What was heavy on land was light in the water, for example. He said that didn't answer his question. He said it didn't come close.

On the day before the town hall meeting, Carl and Celeste arrived at her house at the same time. They tore into each other like feral dogs. Carl straightened his shoulders and said to Alice, "This woman is lying to her own community. The drilling company's not going to repair all the damage they do. After the gas is extracted, after our rivers and streams are polluted, they'll disincorporate and leave." Celeste, facing Carl in the hallway down which Alice hadn't invited them, said, "You need to stop the scare tactics. We have a spotless track record of post-drilling cleanup. What you're saying is libel. We're offering the town a way forward and a chance at a happy future." Alice told them both to leave. She didn't like their screeching. It was inappropriate and painful to hear. She had flushed an off-red, and Carl and Celeste seemed to see her then for the first time.

The problem was simple: no one knew anymore how to behave, what to watch out for, where to turn, or when to obey and when to oppose the forces they would encounter after their bodies ended. The human race had failed to maintain order, and life on Earth was veering dangerously off course. Any almanac could tell you as much. That chaos was gaining the upper hand. The ancients had known better. They had thought that securing this knowledge in the library of Alexandria would protect it. They'd thought—hopefully—that their study of death had domesticated it, had rendered tame the once-wild, and that those who came afterward, the generations watching the Nile overflow its banks every summer, as well as those who sailed across the Mediterranean Sea to populate far-off lands, would benefit. Their descendants wouldn't make the mistake of thinking death unknowable and terrifying. They wouldn't let the subdued grow savage again.

Her parents' final dispute went like this: Alice's father found a dead robin on their doorstep one morning. It seemed at first that a cat had killed and left the robin there, but not finding puncture marks on its body, he figured it had flown into the door and broken its neck. With the body in such good shape, he took it to a taxidermist to have it stuffed. He couldn't later tell Alice why. It just seemed like the right thing to do. For a small extra fee, the taxidermist mounted the bird on a petrified twig soldered to a brass base, which her father took home and placed on the living room mantel. Her mother noticed it the next day while removing pillow covers from the couch. She suffered what felt to her like a mild heart attack. The taxidermist had enlarged and lacquered the bird's eyes so that they exploded from their sockets, and he'd puffed up its bright orange breast to give it a bloated, sexual quality. When she recovered, Alice's mother put on dishwashing gloves and threw it away. Her father returned the next morning to the taxidermist and bought a pre-stuffed titmouse that he placed where the robin had been. His wife promptly disposed of it. This went on for several weeks, with neither Alice's mother nor father speaking about their daily ritual of replacing and discarding stuffed birds, until finally her mother flew to her aunt's in Santa Fe, never to return.

Recently, mummies had been taken from pyramids and sent all over the world on tour, as silent, motionless performers. They were ancient Egyptian royalty deified while alive. Their bodies were small, five feet two inches at most. No one worshipped them now. The attitudes were these: *How could people have thought this little man was a god? What a lot of gold around him! It's too much, except for the scepter and the headdress, which really are impressive.*

On the day of the town hall meeting, Alice arose early and sat on her back porch while orioles scouted for grubs on the banks of the stream. A cat came and crouched in the grass nearby, as still as a statue, and she got up slowly and crept over to it. Like a puff of black smoke, the cat seemed suspended between one state of matter and another. Reaching down she half expected her hands to pass through it; instead the cat spun around and, wild from the lock of her thumbs around its front legs, scratched and bit the inside of her left forearm. She didn't cry out, just stood up and marched with it back into the house, where she threw it in the bedroom closet.

She had not touched her shared bank account with Marouf. Their apartment was in his name. Her father had stayed with them for a week after her mother left, then gone to North Carolina, where his other child lived. She had forgiven the men who'd crashed into her with their truck. They had been drunk and the road slick and she unlucky. This other child, her half-brother, had two young sons who knew someone else as their paternal grandfather, and cats disliked water because water came from Nu, was a projection of Nu, which swelled with the addition of each newly released *ka* and would someday envelop paradise, the home of cats and ancients and Osiris and Isis and Ishtar and Ra.

From behind the closet door, the cat meowed angrily. Alice pressed a paper towel against the ribbons of blood on her arm. The desert around Santa Fe was among the driest places in the country, but her mother liked it, and Marouf would get over her, because although most people were distracted by the earth's skin and no longer knew how to maintain order, the question of good and evil could still be heard if you listened closely enough. It sounded like *Ba ka ba ka ba ka?*

Alice's arm throbbed dully. The cat quieted down. Pain used to be a signal for its host to attend to an injury or surrender to it. Now pain could be a fenced-off abyss, ignored. She knocked on the closet door with her good arm. The cat grew louder.

A list of Alice's good and evil might include the following: misjudging someone at work and getting them fired, telling a friend a harmful truth, leaving her parents to carry on without the balm of her presence, turning inward and away from Marouf, quitting microbiology in college, breaking a boy's heart in front of others in high school, keeping her eyes open while counting in Mandrake Woods, and crying like a baby, unable to see beyond what was missing.

Alice turned the closet doorknob and the cat sprang out and onto the bed. It stalked back and forth on straight legs, its tail curved up sharply. The hair on its face was singed, that on its stomach was matted down as though wet. Alice's heart beat quickly. She'd never been alone with a cat. The sea beneath Mandrake Woods was vast and threatening. Carl and Celeste had left the day before thinking that she, and not they or the interests they represented, needed help. *Ba ka ba ka ba ka?* was babble to them. To most people. She hadn't eaten anything but crackers in a long while, and on her desk lay a letter listing the back taxes owed on her property, which neither she nor her parents could pay. The cat made a guttural cry as if something was lodged in its throat. She could sell the house or sell gas conveyance rights to the drilling company. She could try for restoration.

The cat was clearly sick. It displayed the symptoms of an illness, rabies perhaps. People still died of that. Alice picked it up off the bed and went outside to the stream bank. Her house from this position looked stable, but the support beams in the back were buckling. Marouf had seen it just after they got married and said, *If we were different people, I'd say we should fix the place up and live here.* He was always saying things like that, always suggesting that he and she were set, immutable, ready to be preserved in amber. The sun overhead was a brilliant gold disc pushed across the sky every day by Ra so that people could see what they were doing. But seeing hadn't been enough. Alice made a complete revolution, surveying a landscape she'd come to know late in life. To disinfect a wound, you submerged it in water, the same substance that caused mold and decay and would eventually drown the eternal paradise of the gods. In fact, you lay your whole body down in it. You could do it with a cat held tight to your chest; cats had fallen over time even further than human beings had. You closed your eyes and didn't confuse this with a cleansing or baptism or accident of history. You'd sleepwalked to this edge and there was no escaping what lay beyond, and no use trying, and if only those you loved knew as much. If only it wasn't too late and you could think, for just a moment, that from this pool of fire you might emerge whole again.

THE STRANGER

Mia invited Roger to her rented cabin in the Rocky Mountains to advise her on a screenplay about a jaded stuntman's affair with a troubled schoolteacher. She offered him $5,000. Roger, who'd shattered his ankle the previous October while filming in New Mexico when his horse had a heart attack, and who'd worked since then as a nightclub bouncer in Philadelphia stopping fistfights and dance-floor blow jobs, flew out a week later.

"There's a couple I want you to meet before they go on vacation," said Mia after picking him up at the small regional airport, as they switchbacked along a narrow mountain road with dented guardrails. "Donvieve and Generro. They're old friends of mine who made money from wind farms and are coming in as producers."

Roger quietly took a Vicodin and gazed down at the valley below, a patchwork quilt of ranch squares stiched together by unbending roads and streams. It looked like the kind of landscape quilt a giant might wrap around his shoulders on a cool autumn night when the question of what would happen to him in his declining years, without friends or family to take care of him, would weigh heavily on his mind.

"It's boring here," said Mia, who was forty-three and wore black fishnet stockings, a black miniskirt with toreador threadwork, a black shawl and silver onyx earrings, and had a spiderweb tattoo spun around her neck, "but the seafood's amazing. I'll take you to this tuna place'll blow your mind." The radio station they were listening to became crenellated static. She touched the volume button but didn't turn it down. "Generro's niece is going to house-sit for them while they're away. She just got back from an au pair year in Switzerland and wants to become a nun."

Roger noticed a pen stain on his left pant leg, although he didn't use pens.

Mia tapped him on the wrist. "I said she wants to be a nun."

"Who does?"

"Generro's niece, Anne. I saw you just now. Don't tell me you've become a pill head. That won't work."

"They're for my ankle, from the surgery."

"I thought you had that six months ago."

Roger shook his head. "It wasn't six months ago."

It had been eight months since his ankle surgery, which had gone smoothly and left no lasting damage. He was subletting his Philadelphia apartment to an Argentine scholar, an authority on the failure of American soft power in South America, who'd said when they met to discuss Roger's building and transfer keys, *You look familiar, like I don't know who, but somebody.* The clouds overhead were the color of soapy dishwater that had been sitting in the sink for days because one felt such Vicodin-based calm that one didn't bother draining it. Roger stared up at them, at the clouds, and the bottom of his visual field was perforated by craggy mountains and spiky trees and slender buttes with ivory snowcaps, like a row of shark teeth.

Mia shifted into a lower gear. "We'll be at Donvieve and Generro's in five minutes."

"We're going there now?" He opened his eyes wide and turned his head. "I'm too tired to meet anyone."

"You're just stoned. Have some air." She rolled down his window and the pressure inside the car dropped, as in a small airborne plane when its loading door is pried open. Roger's hair flew out of its careful side part and the radio static was drowned out by the wind's legato bass. Then they reached level ground and passed mock Bavarian castles and geodesic domes honeycombed with solar panels, before turning into the driveway of a blue Tudor cottage.

Anne answered the front door. "They left an hour ago," she said.

"Did they?" Mia frowned. "This is my friend Roger. I'll just use the bathroom, if you don't mind."

Anne shrugged and Mia padded down the hallway. Roger examined a pair of cross swords mounted on the foyer wall, heraldic items with light, elegant etchings, and he needed the $5,000 to pay off his brother, Alfonse, who'd loaned him money for his move from Los Angeles to Philadelphia at six percent interest, which seemed like a lot but was less than Alfonse would have charged if they hadn't been brothers. Anne waited with Roger in order to keep him company, or to make sure he didn't steal anything, or because she'd just been on her way out and couldn't leave until he and Mia left first. Lightning flashed outside and Roger put his hands in his pockets to roll two pills between his thumb and forefinger, tiny wheels going nowhere.

Back in the car ten minutes later, as they accelerated onto a two-lane country highway and rain started to fall, he said to Mia, "I don't think the stuntman character should be jaded. That makes him sound like a private detective. Maybe he could be paranoid from old concussions, but not jaded."

They hit eighty and flew past a team of bicyclists in brightly colored outfits clustering tightly together, like tropical fish at a shark's approach.

"You didn't talk to Anne," Mia said.

"Watch out for the blind curve coming up."

"When I went to the bathroom, you didn't say a word to her."

"The road's getting slick."

Mia brought them down to thirty-five and Roger felt a mixture of relief and disappointment. She said, "You never ignore pretty girls like that," while he took two Vicodins because the last one had had no effect, either because of the altitude or because he'd finally built up too high a tolerance or because Mia's nervous energy was infectious.

"I'm getting married," he said.

"Jesus."

"To Amber. We're doing it in Maine next year on the coast. You should come and bring Brody, if you guys're still together."

The tires hissed on the wet asphalt like a gramophone between songs, and the beetle-ravaged aspen trees on either side of the road were white stalks striped with ribbons of dark brown, standing ramrod straight.

"You know this already," Mia said, "but Amber's wrong for you."

Roger shook his head again. "We never argue. We don't even disagree about anything."

"That's not compatibility. That's not caring."

"What we—" He would have said that respecting someone else's opinions was different than ignoring them, that open-mindedness wasn't apathy, but they were pulling up to Mia's cabin, which was actually an alpine chateau in the Swiss style, with six bedrooms and two hot tubs and a mud room wallpapered an electric orange that gave Roger a headache, or contributed to the headache that had been building for some time. He went to his room, popped four Vicodins, put his phone to sleep, and stared at a water stain on the room's ceiling until it turned invisible.

Over the next week, they spent every morning walking through fields of mountain iris and golden banners, talking about the stunt-man character—he'd have left Hollywood because of a hamstring injury and be working as a bartender, drinking too much, sleeping with whomever was left at the bar at closing time, and fighting with his neighbor about her loud, angry Labradoodle—before going to Donvieve and Generro's house in the afternoon, where Anne would be lying poolside, bored by something on her phone, gloomy because she'd been alone all day, annoyed at having to entertain Mia and Roger again, or brooding over her decision to become a nun. Each time he saw her, Roger thought of fairytale heroines who in pursuit of love gave up a vital part of themselves—their voice or home or identity— and wondered what it felt like to want something that much.

One early evening, Mia left Donvieve and Generro's house to pick up tuna dinners for them in town and called twenty minutes later to say that her car wouldn't start and that she didn't know when she'd be back. Setting down his phone, Roger rose from a plastic pool chair that left bright pink bands on the backs of his thighs and crossed the tiled patio—a fantasia of navy blues, bantam reds, and mossy greens—to get a glass of lemonade from the wheeled drinks cart.

"Her car broke down?" said Anne, removing her sunglasses, on her back on a purple towel. "It's a brand-new rental."

"She's an aggressive driver." Roger added ice cubes and sipped the lemonade and considered telling Anne what he thought was really going on, that Mia wanted them to sleep together so she could write about it in her screenplay. Instead he said, "If me and Amber get a dog, should we get a puppy or a rescue?"

Anne put her sunglasses back on. "Just have a kid already. You're old enough."

"We're not having kids." He returned to his chair, crossed his legs and took no pleasure from hearing the ice cubes tinkle in his glass. "Too expensive." He traced the scar along his left ankle and took a small handful of Vicodins. The actor for whom he'd done the most stunt double work—a muscular, well-hydrated star in his late twenties—had once said to him under a burning October sun after they'd hiked to the top of Runyon Canyon, as distant wildfire smoke billowed into a mottled Los Angeles sky, that he didn't have real conversations with people anymore. No genuine interactions. His, the star's, celebrity scrambled the behavior of everyone he talked to, made them laugh too loudly at his jokes and agree with whatever he said. Sometimes the star met people who, because they too were stars or had heard him complain about never being contradicted, would contradict him, but those occasions also felt unreal. The star was from Indiana, not far from where James Dean had grown up, an actor who'd been unprepared for the hollow freedoms of California. Roger listened and then said that all conversations involved posturing and pretense, so the star wasn't missing out on anything. *Real conversations don't exist*, Roger said. The star looked at him with studied or actual alarm, and said, *That's a jaded thing to say.* Although Roger had only been trying to make the star feel better and didn't actually disbelieve in real conversations, he turned away from his handsome reflection, from someone who could afford everything but what he most needed, and said nothing contradictory.

Anne hadn't wanted to see the Mile High Repertory Theatre's production of *The Miracle Worker* because she already knew too much about Helen Keller's life, but Mia had begged her to come, so on Friday night she sat between Mia and Roger during the poorly lit production—the lighting recreated, to a degree, Helen's visual impairment, with the stage so dark that actors blurred together in places—and then outside the theater, as the audience filed out squinting in the streetlamps' glare, Mia got a phone call and said she'd catch up with them for dinner at the tuna place around the corner, La Mer.

But La Mer was closed for a private party, so Anne and Roger went to a Mediterranean bistro nearby and ordered falafel sandwiches from a teenager with a chin-strap beard, nose ring, foundation makeup, gold hoop earrings, Denver Broncos cap, shiny marcelled hair, white button-up blouse, pomegranate lip gloss, and teardrop tattoo at the corner of his right eye. The teenager said, glancing at a TV monitor mounted on the wall, at an ice skating competition with sequined skaters in love, "I'll bring out your order when it's ready."

At a small vinyl booth, Anne unfolded her napkin and Roger talked about his deaf cousin, Sam, who as a teenager had been swimming off the Jersey Shore when someone spotted a great white shark in the water. The lifeguard on duty ran up and down the beach shouting for everyone to come out, but Sam, not hearing, continued to float on his back.

Their sandwiches arrived and Anne looked at a whorl of gray in Roger's brown beard, like a satellite photo of a hurricane over land, and said, "Then what happened?"

Roger took a bite. "Nothing."

"The shark didn't attack him?"

"No."

"And he didn't see it?"

"No."

She stopped herself from asking what the point of his story was. Not because it brought into relief the hidden dangers that everyone lived with but few recognized, and not because it resembled a Christian parable or Buddhist koan or other accordion-shaped riddle, and not because she suspected that Roger didn't have a point—maybe he did, maybe he didn't—but because an image came to her of a boy lying out in the serene Atlantic, facing the sky as a cold gray body passed beneath him, in silent conversation with himself or God about the nature of buoyancy.

She covered her falafel with yogurt sauce as a Lebanese marching song played over the sound system. The teenager wiped down the table next to them slowly, as if applying varnish.

Roger said, "My aunt was a nun, Aunt Miriam. She ran marathons and placed in the top five for her age group a few times."

There was something off about the falafel despite the yogurt sauce. Or because of it. Anne spat into her napkin and said, "She must've been a lay sister."

"Is that different from a regular nun?"

Anne nodded. Before leaving for her au pair year in Switzerland, she had contracted with Horst and Inga Mendelssohn, married gynecologists, to take care of their three-year-old, Rebecca, from eight to five Mondays through Fridays, but when she arrived and saw that the Mendelssohns put Rebecca in front of the television every night, she wound up watching the girl all the time. Two months later she demanded that they hire a babysitter to help out. They understood but didn't share Anne's concern about Rebecca watching too much television, because she would soon grow out of it and into reading and schoolwork and playtime with friends. Americans, they knew, micromanaged their children's lives, and Anne was naturally a product of her environment, *Just as we are products of* our *environment*, purred Mrs. Mendelssohn, stroking Anne's knee along the grain of her corduroy pants and ending with a soft calf squeeze, which seemed sexual but wasn't. This warm, conciliatory gesture made Anne feel, along with the sunbeam hitting her through the kitchen skylight under which she and the Mendelssohns and Rebecca sat with cold demitasses of espresso, like a cat who rather than whine to escape should lie back and enjoy it.

Being considerate people, the Mendelssohns hired a part-time babysitter and Anne started going out to bars where she met tall, well-groomed Swiss men who bought her stiff drinks and were strenuous in bed—Swiss sex was a kind of calisthenics—as well as rich, stateless twenty-somethings angry that Europe had become so dull and the United States so spoiled, as well as a hippie fringe always on their way to or from a three-day music festival in the Alps or French countryside or former East Berlin.

One night at a Roma crafts fair on the outskirts of Geneva, Anne was by herself smoking a clove cigarette when a woman with long blue hair, Sister Elise, asked her for a light. The similarities between them were uncanny. Anne had run away from home just after her fifteenth birthday, Sister Elise at sixteen; they read manga books but not graphic novels; as kids they'd loved being spun around by their fathers, then rollercoasters, then marijuana, and then heroin and ketamine before realizing that they couldn't remain dizzy and disoriented forever; they ignored politics; they preferred G-spot to clitoral orgasms even though G-spot orgasms were just the climactic sensation of having one's bladder repeatedly poked; they were Geminis; they had long-dead grandparents and severe allergic reactions to bee stings. At one point Anne wondered if all this were a setup, if Sister Elise had researched her beforehand—the world being full of stalkers—but it was nice to have a friend to meet for walks in botanical gardens and on leafy streets that wound up and down steep, brick-laid hills with sweeping views of Lake Geneva and its dandelion sailboats. Sister Elise explained that her vows had been less about loving God—although she expected, over time, to love Him more and more, as in arranged marriages when you came to see profound goodness in someone who'd once been a stranger—than belonging to a community where charity, love, and order were lived practices rather than aspirations. Sister Elise still enjoyed sex sometimes and secular art sometimes, but those things and their pursuit no longer consumed her. They'd become occasional treats, parts of a balancing act instead of obstacles to salvation.

This intrigued Anne, who had always thought, or hoped, that there was a better way to live than what she'd observed growing up, and who worried about what lay before her: community college fol-

lowed by two years at a university where she would train in a com-
petitive field and go into debt, a bold and exciting but difficult and
professionally unfulfilling move to a big city in her mid-twenties,
serio-comic dating in her late twenties, a rationalized marriage in her
thirties to try to beat the biological clock, frustration in her forties
that patterns of behavior repeated themselves so often, resignation in
her fifties to the fact that she would never know anything really and
that her friends were beginning to get sick and die or radically rein-
vent themselves, a stunned and fearful sense of superannuation in her
sixties, renewed resignation in her seventies, a slow-drip senility in
her eighties, and finally a fog of illness and dementia in her nineties
leading to death. So one weekend she visited Sister Elise's monastery,
participated in an evening social, and asked to join.

Anne said to Roger, "Let's not say anything about the falafel."

"What do you mean?"

She pushed her plastic tray to the middle of the table and felt a
trickle of acid reflux and held her breath. The teenager stood next to
them, retying his apron, raptly watching a man and woman sail into
and out of each other's arms. She closed her eyes and this was nothing, a minor trial before the accident of her life assumed the hard
contours of intention.

A week after *The Miracle Worker*, Mia sliced open two bagels and
dropped them in the toaster. Crumbs covered the kitchen counter like
Braille while Roger sat at the breakfast nook with an empty coffee cup.

She said, "Donvieve and Generro are coming back tonight, so I
told Anne she could stay with us till she leaves next week."

"What for? They're her aunt and uncle."

"Donvieve and Generro are very private people." Mia spread
Philadelphia brand cream cheese on the bagels and sat at the breakfast nook and pushed a plate toward Roger.

"I'm not going to sleep with her," he said.

The first movie Mia directed, *Wild Ride High*, had been a hit teen dramedy that launched careers and catchphrases and a national conversation about adolescent desire, idealism, and kill-everyone alienation. Her parents, professors at a small liberal arts college in Memphis, had tried to hide their disappointment in it, her father saying, "The soundtrack was well chosen, all diegetic," and her mother saying, "It's not your average teen exploitation," but she cried after talking to them and started adapting *A World of No Consequence*, the 1916 Austrian classic they'd made her read in high school. While writing the second scene, in which Herr Stroheim, a low-level diplomat, is invited to dinner by copper magnate Christoph von Richter ("Someday copper will replace every other kind of wire," says von Richter during his unannounced visit to Herr Stroheim, who's depressed because he's being sent to the Austrian embassy in Argentina after having fallen in love with a married woman and fathered a child with his housekeeper and gotten syphilis from a prostitute), and anticipates a long night of dull small talk and hysteria over Britain's naval maneuvers in the Strait of Gibraltar, as happens at every dinner party these days, and so tries to get out of the invitation by confiding his problems to von Richter ("You mean you haven't had syphilis since you were twelve?" cries von Richter, wiping sweat from his high, shiny forehead. "And this is your only bastard child? And to love a married woman, what's better? She's already paid for and can't complain about your dalliances. You're the luckiest man in Vienna!"), Mia got a call from her agent excited over the weekend grosses for *Wild Ride High*. Did she, Mia, want to direct a talking dog comedy with two of the biggest actors in Hollywood for a million dollars? Sitting in her tiny, un-air-conditioned bungalow, Mia fingered her copy of *A World of No Consequence* and asked if the talking dog script was good. *A couple more drafts*, said her agent, *and it's a family favor-*

ite. But it would never be one of Mia's family's favorites, so she told him about *A World of No Consequence*, and he said that after doing *Here Comes Trouble!* she'd have the clout for any passion project she wanted.

"Anne's serious about her vows," Roger said, "and I respect that."

The talking dog movie had made money, but Mia still couldn't make *A World of No Consequence*—no one wanted to finance a WWI-era period piece set in Central Europe without sex or violence, and no one ever would—so she directed *Here Comes Double Trouble!* and *Here Comes Trouble 3: Raise the Woof!*, on the set of which she met Roger and her soon-to-be-ex-boyfriend, Brody. When the second sequel did poorly and the franchise went on hiatus, Mia brainstormed original story ideas until a mutual friend told her that Roger had left the stuntman profession after breaking his ankle because he was fed up with staged fighting and staged courage and staged pain—he hadn't said as much, but how else could you account for his move back to Philadelphia?—and she went to Colorado and invited him to join her as a consultant.

"Plus," said Roger, "I couldn't do it to Amber. We're supposed to be monogamous."

"I don't want you to sleep with Anne," said Mia.

"You don't?"

She shook her head.

"It seems like you've been trying to get us together, since we go over there every day, and all the car trouble and phone calls."

"You're being paranoid."

Before Roger could answer, Mia told him about Samara, the second unit director on *Here Comes Trouble 3: Raise the Woof!*, who was fighting stage three breast cancer with a strict diet of dark-hued berries and tempeh tacos, and who, too weak to work, lay on her couch all day taking virtual tours of the world's Seven Wonders. Mia had seen her a month before and they'd watched extraordinary aerial footage of Machu Picchu together, and Samara's husband was no help, had collapsed in the face of her illness and was probably having a midlife crisis. Roger stopped trying to interject.

Later that afternoon they picked up Anne and went to dinner at La Mer, which had run out of tuna but had a superb special, shark fin soup, which all three ordered, and Roger didn't look at or talk to Anne, and then back at the cabin Mia put her on the third floor, in a bedroom directly above his. Either he would hear Anne's footsteps and go up and ask her to walk more quietly, say *Let me show you what I mean* and enter her room and see her clothes strewn about, or he'd stay in his own bed all night, inhibited from visiting her by the squeaky steps between the second and third floor. Mia sat in her study and didn't call Brody, who'd said before she left for Colorado that he wanted to be with someone more dynamic, which meant younger. She'd expected it from him. Some people, you knew right away what they'd do in the end. The arc of their lives had been drawn many times before and you just had to ask yourself whether the design, however familiar, was worth living with for a while. She heard a squeaky step.

Two years later Mia's movie premiered at a small theater in downtown Los Angeles that normally screened independent documentaries and curated double features. Roger flew into LAX beforehand and took a train through neighborhoods once known for drive-by shootings and malt liquor and elementary school metal detectors, now with inspirational murals and after-school tutoring programs and freshly painted porch swings. It was the kind of cityscape a giant wouldn't touch, knowing that once he made peace with being alone, he'd be free. Roger met Anne at a coffee shop on Broadway and learned that Mia was running late and wouldn't see them until after the premiere.

Over weak green tea Anne told him that college was hard because her major, marine biology, required time-consuming fieldwork, but overall she enjoyed it more than she'd thought she would. He told her that his marriage had ended. She was sorry to hear it. It was okay, he said, really, because every divorce was for the best, unlike every marriage. They left the coffee shop and joined the actors, journalists, editors, and industry flacks filing into the theater, where they sat and declined bottled water, and the lights dimmed.

The movie, in black and white, opened on a farm where a young woman lived with her sisters. Their father was often away and they had no mother. Every morning they milked cows, chopped wood, tended a garden, mended clothes, cooked, sang madrigals, and prayed for their father. One day a stranger knocked on the door when the young woman was working alone inside, and said his horse had broken its leg and he was far from home and could he impose on her kindness for a cup of water? She invited him in and said he could stay the night. He would have to be quiet, though, because if her sisters knew he was there they'd tell her father, who would send her away and kill him. The stranger, who had been smiling gratefully, turned pale and asked why she would make him such an offer. Because, she said, it obeyed the natural law of charity and answered the purpose of her father's farm. Why procure milk and firewood and vegetables, why make clothes and meals and music, and why pray for her father if not to share his bounty? Wind through an open window blew the stranger's hair out of its careful side part, and he said that obeying the natural law of charity and answering the purpose of her father's farm were pointless if it cost her her home and him his life. The young woman folded her hands on the table, and the man rose and went to the door. *Aren't you tired of being afraid?* she asked, staring straight ahead. *We're deaf and blind because that's how they want us to be, because that's how they are, but we can be different.* The stranger walked outside and shut the door behind him. The clouds overhead were the color of slurry. He went to the gate, on the other side of which was the path that had brought him there, and then stopped and turned around and walked back to the house.

By now people in the audience were checking their phones and whispering and going to the bathroom. Roger, jetlagged, closed his eyes and opened them when the credits were rolling up the screen, to polite applause. The lights came on and Mia walked onto the stage for a conversation with a local film critic. The critic was reminded of Bergman's medieval allegories and Ibsen's proto-feminist dramas, and yet the movie struck him as essentially a comedy, despite its dark tone and texture, and despite all the deaths in the end. Roger remembered reaching the third floor of Mia's Colorado cabin, and Anne looking down the hallway and asking him to help unzip her suitcase because it was stuck. The critic wondered how Mia felt about releasing something so unlike her past work, with such—to be frank—modest commercial prospects, and Roger had struggled with the zipper and Anne had sat on her bed in a pair of boxing shorts and a sleeveless T-shirt that read *I won't be long*. Mia had disliked commercial success, so she was ready for whatever reception her new film got. Anne had scooted off her bed and dropped slowly to the ground, as though kneeling for a benediction, and Roger had felt in his pockets and found them empty, which hadn't mattered, for the pills no longer worked, and the house had been silent except for their breathing. The critic asked what Mia wanted people to take away from the film. *Take away?* she said. *Nothing. Or that real life is less frightening than fairy tales. And less exciting. And there's no way to know which is better.* Roger leaned over to say something to Anne, but saw that he didn't have to.

HALEY

Forty miles southeast of Philadelphia, Michael owned a large Dutch Colonial house on twenty acres with a pool and private beach access, which he'd bought cheap as an investment when its last occupants, a three-wife, fifteen-child family, were raided in a government crackdown on polygamy. He lived in New York, so it sat empty most of the time.

One summer an artist whose paintings he had collected, Juan, called and asked to stay in it. He'd lost his studio space and had a deadline coming up. Michael looked at the oil painting by Juan on his library wall, a man pruning roses while lava spilled out of a volcano in the background.

"Someone's already there till the end of next month. Let me think, because she's got to focus and I told her she'd have privacy. But you're married now, right? If you and your husband slept in the guest apartment on the third floor and left her alone, it's got a separate entrance and that could work."

Juan and Kyle showed up the next afternoon in a 1979 MG coupe convertible with bucket seats and a sun-bleached Naugahyde interior. Juan's thick black bangs usually fell in a curtain over his eyes, but the drive had blown them into a mess of layered chevrons. He lit a cigarette and felt a tightness in his smoothly shaved chest. The final mile of the trip—on a private dirt road checkered with potholes, past a dried-up pond and grove of bony poplars—had covered him in a thin layer of dust, and he looked like a bronze statue coming to life.

Slumped low in the passenger seat, feet propped against the cracked dashboard, Kyle held a wedge of turkey ham and removed his aviator sunglasses. He turned down the radio's throbbing dance music.

"We're supposed to mow the lawn?" He panned left to right. "It's not a lawn. It's a field."

"And clear the roof gutters of leaves and debris." Juan pulled the loose emergency brake until he felt a faint click. "They get clogged in the rain and erode the tiles."

"Jesus." Kyle massaged the back of his neck, squinting at the roof. "If one of us has to climb a ladder up there, I don't know if you know I get vertigo. It's why I never use escalators. What are the girl's jobs?"

Juan shrugged.

"Does she cook?"

"No idea."

"But we can't talk to her."

"That's right."

The two men got out and stretched. Juan, olive-skinned, long and lean, with the high cheekbones and dark, deep-set eyes of a silent film star; Kyle shorter, fair and sandy-haired, like a mature schoolboy with full, sensuous lips. They were both thirty-six years old. A bald eagle circled overhead, looking for slow rodents in the tall grass.

Kyle slid the turkey ham into a Ziplock. "The third-floor windows don't have curtains. Light's going to flood our room in the morning."

"We'll get on a country rhythm," Juan said. "Go to bed at sunset and wake up at dawn." He'd thought bald eagles were extinct. Had the future predicted by the popcorn epics of his childhood, in which scientists could use DNA samples to bring species back, already arrived?

"I could write a note to the girl and see if she cooks."

Juan dropped his cigarette and crossed the driveway to a set of metal stairs zigzagging up to the third-floor guest entrance. He paused on the lanai to catch his breath. Inside he passed through a low-ceiling parlor and lower-ceiling kitchen to a bedroom with jungle-print wallpaper and a four-poster brass bed, Indian rug, mahogany dresser, roll-top desk, and hourglass vanity, the kind of Victorian time capsule that excited and terrified small children.

The problem with the future wasn't just how it changed you, how it replaced what worked with what didn't, but that it kept becoming the present, like magic in reverse. He started to unpack.

Kyle walked in. "You're taking the top drawer?"

Juan scooped up his row of shirts and moved them to the bottom of the dresser.

"I'll bet this place has lead paint," said Kyle. "An old building where no one lives year-round, there's probably asbestos behind the walls. And black mold."

"If you want to complain all month about a free beach house, don't."

"It's not free when we have chores."

Juan had brought too few cigarettes in an effort to force himself to smoke less. The rug featured a daisy chain of elephants in bright red pashminas, trunks and tails tied together. He tried to count them but lost his starting place.

"My friend got scratched by a bat in a house like this last year and had to get rabies shots in her stomach," Kyle said. "I mean the needle was three inches long. Bats can slip through any opening, no matter how small, by liquefying their bones."

"That's not true."

"I think it might be."

"And doctors don't give you rabies shots in the stomach anymore. They do it in the shoulder."

Juan lay back on the bed and ignored his rapid heartbeat. In one version of the future he would find love and get out of debt and stop lying to others to get what he wanted. In another, he would die alone, forgotten, broke, and hungover in Kensington, the heroin capital of the Delaware Valley.

"I should take a shower," he said.

"Want me to join you?"

Juan looked out the window. The bald eagle swooped down from the sky at a kite-string angle, then rose up with a wild hare pumping its long legs and short arms.

"No," he said.

Juan didn't make any progress on his painting during the first few days. It was for a fall show called "Then Everything Changed" at the Ortlieb Gallery, one of the few Philadelphia spaces of which non-Philadelphians had heard. Mornings he sat in the detached four-car garage with a roll of crepe paper and a box of colored pencils, sketching ideas he later rejected as too easy or too hard. After a heavy lunch of turkey ham and farmer's cheese, he'd move to the bedroom and continue making no progress until evening, when Kyle would show up and put on loose silk pajamas and play Majorcan club music and bop around the room talking about the hot Midwestern transplants who got wasted mid-week at Woody's, his neighborhood bar. Eventually Kyle would unbutton his top and scissor his legs back and forth on the bed while Juan sat at his computer reading about the Black Plague, Chernobyl, and the Chicago fire of 1871, and the Dust Bowl, Great Influenza, and Hurricane Katrina, always one or two Internet searches away from the perfect subject.

Kyle saw Haley first, at the beach, piling stones into the belly of her T-shirt, which sagged below her waist so that her bare legs appeared to grow out of thin air.

"Good rocks around here?" he asked, rubbing coconut sunscreen onto his round, freckled shoulders. She was cute in the tomboyish way that semi-straight guys liked—brown bobbed hair, coltish body, cleft chin, and Bambi eyes.

"Yeah, agates."

Kyle tucked the tube of cream into the sideband of his peach swim thong. Tan lines, whether from bronzing spray or real, weren't sexy.

"I don't know what your jobs are, but we're going to hire someone to do yard work before we leave. You could split the cost with us."

She didn't answer, just squatted down and splashed small handfuls of water onto her arms and face, as if having to conserve it, like someone at a desert oasis.

Kyle described this encounter later in the garage while Juan did bench presses. The girl was either retarded, Kyle said, or on heavy drugs, in which case she should share instead of hoarding the fun. The garage had stuffed animals, a ten-gallon deep fryer, softball equipment, a crank-operated ice cream maker, and a ready-to-assemble outdoor gazebo still in its packing crate—everything needed to run a small county fair. It was ninety degrees with the doors up and windows open.

"You're not supposed to talk to her," Juan said.

Kyle looked at the mirrored back of an aluminum BabyKakes sign propped against a pristine push mower and pulled his socks up to his knees.

"There's a ton of algae in the water," he said. "Looks like a big brain floating offshore. No way I'm swimming in it."

"Did you hear me? Leave the girl alone!"

Raising his hands palms out, Kyle made an *Easy, tiger* face and moved around to the foot of the weightlifting bench, blocking the overhead light.

"You're tense these days, you know that? In general you've become a very tense person."

"Michael asked us not to bother her, so we need to respect that."

"I know what you need. To relieve your tension."

With the last of his strength, Juan pushed the barbell up and into its cradle. His arms fell limp to the floor.

"Do you know what it is?" Kyle asked.

The ceiling rafters seemed to expand and contract as nausea and muscle exhaustion and heat fatigue and anxiety hit Juan in waves, like he'd eaten a burrito in the middle of an uphill run on acid.

"I said do you know what it is?"

"What *what* is?"

"What you need to relieve your tension."

"I need to finish my painting."

Kyle shook his head. "Sex. You need sex. And you need it with me."

With his stomach in turmoil, Juan lay still and thought about the Haitian earthquake.

"We talked about the situation before we got here."

"The situation is ridiculous."

"You're getting a vacation out of it."

"I could be at Woody's right now with a bunch of ripped young Vikings instead of playing your beard—for what, exactly? I have needs and you have needs. There's no one here but the girl, and it'd be good if she saw us together, anyway."

A hundred and fifty-nine thousand dead. A quarter million houses destroyed. Thirty thousand commercial and public buildings damaged. People all over the world hadn't known Haiti could be so poor, and aid and volunteers had flowed in, and global consciousness had been raised. But had the earthquake changed anything? Had poverty there or elsewhere ended? Had the line between the First World and Third World blurred? Following the Holocaust everyone had said never again, but then came the Khmer Rouge, and then Rwanda, and soon—

"Is it you think I'm ugly?" Kyle asked.

"No, of course not."

Before running into him at the Reading Terminal Market a month earlier, Juan hadn't seen Kyle since high school. Neither had aged much, but it took a few minutes for them to recognize each other in the small group watching a blender demonstration. Kyle launched into his romantic problems ("It all boils down to men in this city wanting commitment") and professional limbo ("Restaurant managers will fire you now for doing the tiniest bump of coke on the job, no trial, no jury") and housing issues ("I've been staying with friends, but futons are bad for my back"). Juan nodded and got an idea.

"Do you think I'm attractive?" Kyle pushed his blond hair into a cologne ad pompadour and dropped his chin to look at Juan with a supplicating, expectant expression.

"Sure, but I'm not attracted to you."

"You think I'm attractive but aren't attracted to me? That doesn't make any sense. It's like saying you love pizza but don't want to eat it."

"There are a lot of attractive people in the world I'm not attracted to."

"Don't be semantical." Kyle widened his stance until his legs touched Juan's. "Sex is a passageway for creative energy. It's why your painting's not going well. Block off sex and nothing can get through, in or out." He got down on his knees and placed his hands on Juan's legs and rotated his thumbs in quarter-sized circles at mid-thigh, moving slowly upward. "You need to relax."

Juan exhaled loudly and sat up and excused himself to the guest apartment to read about Castle Bravo, the most powerful nuclear device ever detonated by the United States. It had landed on Bikini Atoll in 1954, appeared to military observers like a second sun, irradiated hundreds of Marshall Islanders, and spread fallout across the planet. Yet it, too, hadn't changed anything. People watched Castle Bravo as if it were an Olympic event. Nobody responded like Robert Oppenheimer had to the first atomic bomb test, the Trinity explosion in New Mexico on July 16, 1945, by quoting the *Bhagavad Gita*: "Now I am become Death, the destroyer of worlds."

Juan smoked a cigarette that tasted like fresh cedar, took two antacid tablets, and closed his computer. Besides crickets and the muffled metronome of a grandfather clock from the floor below, the room was silent. In college he'd seen Bruegel's *Landscape with the Fall of Icarus* for the first time, and spent months studying its calm depiction of a man leading his horse and cart along a hilly seaside road while Icarus, having flown too close to the sun, fell into the water behind him. Juan updated its theme and color palette for his final portfolio, a series of paintings that represented people absorbed in minor tasks while large-scale tragedy happened nearby. Beginning at his senior show, he sold everything he'd done to collectors and galleries, and was praised by many critics ("profound juxtapositions of the mundane and the terrible"), and dismissed by a few ("like CGI mockups for bad disaster movies"). Commissions for similar works poured in, and he was content and busy and enjoyed a growing reputation. When he turned thirty, however, his enjoyment faded and he began to worry that he was repeating himself. Friends assured him that artists really only had one subject, and that consistency wasn't the hobgoblin of little minds, but rather the sign of great ones, and he half-believed them until one afternoon in January he had a panic attack in his studio and fell and knocked out a front tooth and decided he could never again portray someone engrossed in an ordinary task against a backdrop of catastrophe.

He didn't know what to paint instead and months passed without him touching his brushes. His bank account dwindled, and in April he had unexpected legal expenses, so by June, when the Ortlieb Gallery promised him $50,000 for a painting in his old style, he felt like an aging, bankrupt middleweight offered a big payday to fight the new world champion, unable to say no.

Kyle still wasn't back at 2 a.m. Juan sent him a text message, rested his head on his arms, and closed his eyes.

A knock on the door late the next morning got Juan up. Haley introduced herself ("like the comet, but spelled with only one ell") and asked if she could borrow his car to go to the supermarket because it took forever to get to town by bus. She wore purple flip-flops, striped baby blue board shorts, a beaded onyx necklace, and an oversized T-shirt that hung off her left shoulder.

Juan apologized for Kyle bothering her the day before and handed her his key.

She thanked him, bounced down a few steps, and then looked back up, a hand shading her dark eyes.

"You have auto insurance, right?"

"Of course."

Her clanging footsteps sent vibrations through the metal staircase when she reached the second-floor landing.

"Wait!" He stepped to the railing. "It's just basic liability, the minimum legal amount."

"Okay."

"Are you a good driver?"

She seemed to think about it. "Yeah."

"Have you ever been in an accident?"

"Yes, but one of them wasn't really my fault. This guy was going so slow through a yellow light that anyone coming through the intersection would've hit him." She turned around reluctantly. "I'll understand if you don't want me using your car."

Juan's canvases were rolled up in tubes in the garage, not stretched out, not primed and not prepped. Had Kyle slept in there, on the fleece pelt Juan used for napping?

He closed the door behind him. "I'll take you. I need to get some things, too."

The nearest town was empty between Labor Day and Memorial Day, but in the summer it swarmed with people buying handheld American flags, sand buckets, insect repellant, candy bracelets, beach permits, infused waters, bloating remedies, condoms, cartoon maps of Delaware, sunglasses, discounted blankets that said *Back that thang up*, spray bottles, flippers, beach balls, plastic sandals, plastic water guns, and gum.

As they drove along Main Street, Haley told Juan that she would be a senior at the state university once she finished three incompletes from last semester—one in organic chemistry, another in biological chemistry, and the third in music appreciation. Her legs were the same olive shade as his, and the V-neck of her shirt reached the middle of her breastbone. She'd chosen chemistry as a major because her aunt worked for a pharmaceutical company in New Jersey and could get her a job. She crossed her legs and Juan tried to count the number of minivans ahead of them. It was impossible. The more she learned about drug research, the less appealing it seemed. It involved so many computational equations, so much careful measuring, and so many blind trials leading only to patentable tweaks on about-to-go-generic drugs. She dreaded it. Dance music pulsed quietly out of the car stereo. What she really wanted was to make jewelry, but if she quit school now she'd have to start paying back her student loans right away.

"Can't Michael give you money?" Juan asked, and was about to suggest that she adjust her shirt when the minivan in front of them, with orange-trimmed Florida plates, stopped to let a pedestrian cross the street. He slammed on the brakes.

"I suppose," Haley said, twirling a strand of hair around her finger and staring at a question traced in dirt on the back of the minivan: *Ask me how I'm changing the environment.* "But that would be weird."

"No, it wouldn't. I'm sure he expects it."

The minivan didn't go forward after the pedestrian reached the sidewalk.

"Why do you say that?" Haley asked.

"Because," said Juan.

From the driver side of the minivan a man about Juan's age, broad-chested and red-faced, wearing a Dolphins visor and a knee brace, got out and examined his back bumper.

"You just hit me?" he asked angrily. "My kids felt something."

"No."

"They said there was a jolt."

"Not from my car."

Haley drew her left foot up and tucked it under her right leg, and looked at Juan.

"Why does Michael expect me to ask for money?"

"Your front end's all scratched up," said the minivan driver.

"That's regular street wear," Juan said. "I live in Philadelphia."

The man pulled the visor down and glanced at Haley.

"Philly, huh. You got a jail at the Eagles stadium for when fans attack other teams' supporters, I heard. What's the deal with that? Why you guys so violent?"

Haley said, "We didn't hit you and you're blocking traffic, so you should get going."

"Yeah, okay." The man didn't look angry anymore, just concerned, like a highway patrolman issuing a warning instead of a ticket. "Football isn't ballet, but still it's got rules. There's kids watch the games. Just relax, is what I'm saying."

He climbed back into his vehicle and drove away.

At the supermarket Haley got a stack of frozen lasagnas and breakfast burritos. Goosebumps flared up and down her arms. Juan filled a basket with turkey ham and farmer's cheese and she asked why he and Kyle didn't wear wedding rings. He said rings were just symbols. She gave him a quizzical look and said she thought the whole point of getting married was symbolism. He said there were a lot of points to marriage and asked why she'd taken so many incompletes. She said it was complicated and grabbed a magazine from the checkout rack featuring an actress whose autoimmune disorder had made her reconsider alcohol, animal testing, and foreign men. "It's a wake-up call," said the cover.

On the drive back, Haley said Juan and Kyle should join her for dinner. He said they were busy and felt lightheaded and almost pulled over twice before they reached the house.

Kyle's things were gone. Juan stared at the empty top dresser drawer in the bedroom, then sat with his sketchpad for several motionless hours, and then started writing an email to the Ortlieb Gallery saying he wouldn't have a painting for its show. He'd tried to find an event that had changed everything, but what looked like historical endpoints always turned out to be pauses before a cycle started over again. Proof was everywhere. God had flooded the Earth in order to wipe out evil forever, for example, but no sooner did the ground dry out than Sodom and Gomorrah sprang up. Juan smoked the butt of yesterday's cigarette—more cedar—and outside a full moon bathed the field in alabaster light. As with concepts like evil, so with concrete phenomena. After the rise and fall of the Roman Empire came the rise and fall of the Ottomans and the Dutch and the British and the Soviets and the Americans. Repetition, repetition, repetition. Juan wished he could give the Ortlieb Gallery something, but—

A burst of laughter downstairs. He quit typing, heard a male voice, and went down to find Haley in the front room with her legs draped over the lap of a young man in a ribbed wife beater and camouflage shorts whose short brown hair lay so flat on his head it looked like a pencil drawing.

"Can I talk to you?" Juan said to Haley.

The young man said, "You one of the gay dudes upstairs?"

"It'll just take a minute."

"You should spin records down here, bro. There's a Technics SL-1210M5G turntable over there. I DJ up the Shore on Tuesdays, but I don't have my vinyl with me, so if you got any Hi-NRG disco, bring it."

Haley followed Juan out to the porch and leaned against the doorjamb and clasped her hands in a choirgirl pose. She was wearing a purple miniskirt and a sparkling black halter top that looked like a band of night sky.

"If we're being too loud, I'll tell Ethan to shut up."

"I thought you were supposed to be studying."

"I needed a break."

"You got a break today when we went to town." Juan detected an unpleasant urgency in his voice, and he stood up straighter. "It's just that Michael probably doesn't want you bringing guys here."

"And he probably doesn't want you lying to him about being married." She stood up straighter, too, as if they were playing Simon Says. "You got divorced a few months ago. I read it online."

Juan looked behind him, as if Michael or his ex or the Ortlieb Gallery manager who'd advertised the show using Juan's name might be standing there, irate and expectant. "I can explain that."

"Okay."

"The only way I could work here was to let Michael think I was still married." He realized what a lame explanation this was, like telling a judge he'd robbed someone for the very good reason that he wanted money. "It won't matter anymore because I'm leaving in the morning."

She tilted her head and they heard rattling and looked over to see Ethan straining to open the window from inside the house. It flew up after a loud crack and the thud of something hitting the floor.

"Cheap lock," he muttered, stepping through the frame. "I just found three copies of *The Sound of Music* behind that hula girl lamp—I'm like, holy shit, three—and some diet Red Bulls and root beer schnapps. And there's a bat in the hallway."

"A bat?" Haley said.

"In the hallway. It's huge."

Juan went to the garage for the pool cleaning net he'd seen beside a gallon of chlorine and box of water toys. It took him a few minutes to drive the bat into the kitchen, where it circled the room inches below the ceiling. He swung and missed several times before Haley, watching it carefully, her head bobbing up and down as if she were about to jump into a game of double Dutch, took the net and in one swoop slammed the animal to the ground. Juan found a paper bag to transport it outside, but when she lifted the net it thrashed around and escaped down the hallway and out the front door.

Ethan's eyes had been closed the whole time. "Who wants a shot of schnapps?" he said.

"I'm tired," said Haley. "Ethan, go home."

———

At 2 a.m. Haley pounded on Juan's door and showed him two marks on her left arm. Full of adrenaline, she hadn't felt the bat scratch her when it happened. He drove her to the hospital, which no longer administered rabies shots and directed them to a nearby non-emergency outpatient clinic. The night receptionist ordered the virus and immunoglobulin serums from a storage facility in Wilmington and told them to sit in the waiting room.

Haley asked Juan why he was leaving in the morning. He told her about the Ortlieb Gallery's show and his failed hunt for the right subject. She asked if he had to interpret "Then Everything Changed" on such a large scale. Instead of a nation's turning point, what if he painted the moment an individual's life changed? Someone falling in love, say, or getting in a bad accident or finding God or walking in on their cheating partner. For the person in question, a boyfriend's betrayal could be as calamitous as an asteroid hitting the planet. Juan said that wouldn't work.

"Why not?" she asked. The scratches on her arm were wide, as if made by human fingernails, and he didn't have an answer.

Later that day Haley gripped Juan's steering wheel with a look of shock and incomprehension on her face, modeling a woman who'd just gotten in a car crash and lost her leg, while Juan sat on a stool in front of his easel sketching and erasing and resketching and painting. During breaks they talked about Haley's jewelry (she favored using simple silver chains and amethysts and carnelian agates) and towns they both knew (she'd grown up in New Hope, Pennsylvania, and he in neighboring Doylestown) and her generation's practicality (everyone's parents had followed their bliss and wound up non-blissful) and his ex (who'd divorced him for, among other reasons, throwing away his career) and Michael's business (financial consulting? Angel investing?) and smoking (there were worse vices, they agreed, lighting up).

At the end of the session she asked to see what he'd done so far, but he never showed anyone a work in progress, and she said that root beer schnapps was foul but it would do the trick, and he said he wanted to finish the painting before they drank together. She didn't understand restraint. It got easier over time, he said. She doubted that very much. He said she was smart to be skeptical.

The next morning Juan heard a scraping sound from the roof. Outside Kyle stood at the top of an extension ladder, scooping out clumps of soil and leaves and dropping them to the ground.

"What are you doing?" Juan shouted.

Kyle looked down. "Clearing the gutters!"

Juan grabbed the base of the ladder. "You shouldn't do that without a spotter! It's dangerous!"

Kyle climbed down a few minutes later in tight hiking shorts with the legs rolled up, a broad-brimmed gardening hat, and a button-up denim shirt. He was sweating heavily. Yes, it was immature to have left without writing Juan a note or responding to his (thoughtful, well-written, and appreciated) text messages, but Kyle had been upset. Although "upset" didn't capture the disappointment and hurt he'd felt, not because of Juan's cruelty or Kyle's wounded vanity—one could not live long without learning to make excuses for unresponsive men—but because he'd discovered something painful during their brief but powerful time together.

Kyle had learned that he was, contrary to his vision of himself as a witty, charming *bon vivant*, in fact lazy and bratty. He understood why Juan had rejected him. Had their roles been reversed—that is, had Kyle been the generous, industrious one in the relationship—he too would have refused the advances of his man-child friend who'd whined constantly about the negligible shortcomings of this beautiful beach house. There came a time in every man's life when he had to admit that he was not perfect—nor anywhere close—and that if he wanted to continue ignoring his flaws he would lose out on the increasingly rare opportunities for romantic happiness that came his way. Kyle would soon be thirty-seven years old. He needed to take responsibility for what had gone wrong in the past and resolve to be a better, kinder, more accepting person. The future, he said, could be whatever he wanted it to be. A place of infinite possibility. He didn't care if this sounded hokey. He, Kyle, was saying that he could and would be different. Not that he expected Juan to process all of this at once and take him right to bed. That might happen in fairy tales, but this was the real world and Kyle had to prove himself. He knew that. Was clearing the gutters a good start? Yes. Was it by itself enough? No. He would mow the lawn next, and then they'd talk about other actions that would speak louder than words.

He set off briskly for the garage.

"Wait a second," said Juan, starting after him. "Let's have coffee and talk upstairs."

Kyle hit the button to open the garage doors, found the push mower and was rolling it out when he stopped abruptly.

"What's this?" he said.

Juan said, "My new painting."

"What's it have to do with 'Then Everything Changed'?"

"A woman has just lost her leg in a car crash. The subject doesn't have to be a major earth-shattering event, but can be on a smaller scale."

"It's the girl."

"Haley's modeling for it, yeah."

"It's just her face. Where's the car crash?"

"I was going to do the whole scene, but then I thought that that would be sensationalistic, and that the subtler thing would be to do a close-up of her just after the accident, as she's comprehending what happened."

"She doesn't look traumatized."

"The brain shuts down pain receptors when it's in shock. This woman has lost her leg but can't feel it yet."

Kyle licked his lips. His chest rose and fell visibly.

"So what looks like a normal portrait of the girl is really a horrible moment when everything's changed for her?"

"Yes."

"That's subtle, all right." Kyle turned from the painting to Juan and his voice was steady and his eyes clear. "And here I thought becoming a better person would impress you. How funny. You're chasing the girlfriend of the friend who launched your career by buying your first paintings, and who's loaning you his house. Doesn't get any worse than that."

Juan heard footsteps behind him.

"Am I interrupting something?" Haley asked.

At the opening of the Ortlieb Gallery's fall show, Juan talked to people about his painting, "Haley." It didn't seem to fit the show's theme or belong to any current art movement, or to any recent or coming school, and so, said these people, its already having sold was surprising. Although its subject, a young woman who looked at once bored and excited, was like all the other bored, excited young women whose faces were used to create and promote and frustrate desire, and was, if one thought about it from one angle but not from another, subversive.

After an hour, Juan looked at his watch and got his coat from the check stand and pulled out a cigarette and was about to leave for the airport, when he felt a hand on his shoulder and turned and saw a man in his early sixties with curly white hair and gold-framed glasses.

"Michael!"

"Are you going somewhere?"

"The airport. I have a ten o'clock flight to Italy."

"Italy!"

Juan nodded and his mouth was dry. He put his hand in his pocket and fingered the smooth agates that had been placed there earlier.

"Like I said on the phone, I'm sorry. It was an accident."

A couple entered the gallery and squeezed between them, the man in a black velvet coat and the woman in a daisy-print sundress.

"You remember when we met, at your senior show in college?" Michael asked. "I hadn't gone there to buy anything, and then I wound up taking home two of your paintings. I'd thought that was an accident, too."

He adjusted his belt, an old leather double-buckle that Juan remembered him buying at an outdoor market in Florence.

"She said you didn't love her," Juan said.

Michael shook his head. "No, I couldn't manage it."

Fifteen years earlier Juan and Michael had sat at a café in the Italian Alps drinking wine by a lake, and Juan had talked for a long time about their future together, and the cities they would live in—New York, Rome, Madrid—until finally Michael put a hand to his mouth and said, "This is a beautiful lake. Let's not neglect it."

The couple that had just come in was now leaving, and they stepped between Juan and Michael again.

"Do you have time for a drink?" Juan asked.

"No," said Michael, "and neither do you. Send me a postcard. Or paint a new portrait of Haley. The one I have could use a companion."

Michael clasped Juan's hand, and then Juan walked outside and closed the door behind him and in the distance heard gunfire, unless it was fireworks, and he fingered the agates in his pocket as he hailed a cab and wondered if Haley, at the airport just then, would decide they were all the same.

ARISING

The tiger stopped at a break in the rain and realized he was no longer on the path he'd been following. He scratched the side of his belly against a coleus bush, shook free of the water coating his back and legs, and studied the ferns and mosses growing all around him, a blurred patchwork of greens. He listened for the rasp of Cousin, which like a gnat's buzzing at his tail had annoyed him all through the hunt, and for the whelps of Sister's underweaned cubs, and for the irregular footsteps of Second Cousin, but heard nothing.

"I'm six furlongs west of the den," he thought, catching the scent of the dead opossum. "At most nine."

He was tempted to scoop up with his tongue an ant dragging a webbed mass of tsetse flies, but refrained. What could be seen of the sun seemed to shift and ripple in the sky like its reflection in disturbed water. Was he west of the den, or north? Perhaps he was northwest. Cousin, despite his uselessness in a kill, had a perfect sense of direction, and the tiger felt his absence. Not long ago, for example, Cousin had found the way home after a two-day journey through alien trees that had marooned them in an unfamiliar glade, where they were so famished that Aunt had proposed eating Second Cousin.

"Sister!" he called out. "Niece!"

The chittering whir of life in the forest slowed and then sped up again.

"Can I help you?" came a voice from above.

The tiger looked up and saw a snake wound around the gnarled branch of a tree that curved at its base into thick tumorous roots burrowing underground. "Yes, you can go up to a good vantage point and look east for a pride of six tigers. One has a limp, another is missing both ears, and a third has no tail."

The snake's mouth opened slightly.

"They can't be more than a furlong away. Maybe two."

After making a complete revolution around its branch, the snake glided toward the trunk and then up to another branch. "What happened to your left eye?"

"It was removed by a great rhinoceros. You're not high enough there to see any real distance." The tiger sat on his haunches and felt the sharp pain in his groin that had troubled him since the last famine. He covered the furless patch on his stomach with his right foreleg, and the long, sparsely plotted whiskers on his face hung like wilted plume grass. "The rain must have disoriented them. They'll be desperate to find me. Second Cousin already suffers from nerves. Go to the topmost branch and scan the area and you are sure to spot them."

The snake projected a third of its body into midair and peered up at the tumescent sky. "There is an eagle circling."

"You are too large to be carried off by such a small bird."

"Just as you are too powerful to be maimed by a rhinoceros?"

The tiger considered leaping up to seize the snake in his mouth but suspected, with his injury, that he couldn't.

The snake remained motionless.

"If you don't help me," said the tiger, "I will find them on my own and then return to kill you."

With its tail the snake plucked an apple from a leafy nest and squeezed until it liquefied and streamed to the ground. "Before you arrived, I saw six tigers to the southeast, standing in an attitude of respect around a young tiger half again your size. When he trotted away they followed him in single file, and there were a tailless male and limping female among them."

The tiger protracted his claws deep into the earth and objects around him grew less distinct. His heart beat erratically. "You saw a different pride that coincidentally and superficially resembled mine."

"Yes, certainly."

"There is no possibility of one being the other."

"I didn't mean to suggest there was."

After a minute in which he shivered as if still wet—a ringing in his inner ear, a cold hard trill, made him wish for the sun's full return—the tiger squinted at the snake and said, "You are lying about what you saw. It is your nature to trick noble animals, as you did man."

The snake dropped what remained of the apple to the ground, where it landed on a pile of rotting cores around which flies were buzzing ecstatically, and slid down to hang suspended with its tail coiled around a short spiky branch. Up close the tiger could see its skin reticulated into a network of fitted, glistening scales that were honeycombed with tiny red diamonds. A change occurred in the opossum scent; a new bloody aroma mingled with the old decay, as though its body had just been torn open; he could almost hear skin being ripped away and flesh stripped from bone.

"I will not tell—"

"How old are you?" asked the snake.

"I will not tell you again: either go up and look for my companions or prepare to die."

"You shouldn't blame them for following another tiger now that you can no longer procure food or protect them."

The tiger rose from his seated position and paced back and forth unsteadily, trying to determine how high he could jump without further straining his groin muscle. If the snake descended another two branches and then lowered its head and relaxed, he'd have a chance. "I can procure enough food for twenty tigers; at this very moment I am hunting prey. As for guarding them against danger, in the last six months I have fought off two jackals, a wombat, a marbled cat, an olingo, and a sambar deer. The few among my pride who have been injured during that period understand why I was unable to prevent it, such as, during our encounter with the rhinoceros, my own loss of an eye. They are loyal in a way that you, a solitary creature hated the world over, cannot understand."

The snake seemed to consider this. "I wonder how a sambar deer, or a marbled cat or an olingo, could threaten a tiger. An olingo! The smallest cub could swallow one whole without thinking. Though the real question here is why your pride has waited so long to abandon you."

The tiger sprang up at the tree from a meter away, felt a sharp bolt of pain, and fell to the ground.

The snake said, "Despite your obvious helplessness, if your former pride comes this way its new leader will have to kill you. The old must ever make way for the young."

The tiger turned away and tensed his muscles and clenched his jaw and didn't make a sound. From between his legs agony radiated out in regular, insistent waves. It would soon subside. He watched a chameleon blend into a fern stem as hardy as a shoot of running bamboo; the wind moaned and the sky darkened two shades with the sun's full retreat behind layered clouds. He felt a drop of rain, heavier and more deliberate than any in the shower that had fallen earlier. The opossum scent was faint. He said, "I look forward to meeting this other tiger. Before ending your life, I will beat him in front of you so that you can see your error."

The snake plucked off another apple and reduced it, as he had the one before, to pulp. "Let us stop this absurd talk of you harming me, because the only animal you can hurt now is yourself. It would be best for you to accept this and everything to follow."

The tiger said, "Do you want to know why you are everywhere despised?"

The snake said nothing.

"It isn't just your willful insincerity, the way you manipulate the truth and consider honesty to be a sign of mental frailty, as though animals who treat each other fairly are too stupid to do otherwise, but rather that, unable to build anything yourself, you concentrate on destruction. I almost pity you."

"Then we might start a mutual pity society."

"Friendless, heartless, and deluded into thinking cleverness worthier than love and affection, you could vanish and no one would miss you."

The snake's head rested on its coiled body, ten feet off the ground. "And how are you any better off, since your life has come to the same solitary end?"

"I am not solitary or at an end."

The snake looked meaningfully at the empty space around the tiger. "It's especially unfortunate because your solitude is not the result, as mine is, of your possessing taste and refinement in a place that values neither, but because when young you used brute force to dominate all the creatures of the earth. Those you didn't eat you frightened, displaced, or ignored. How love and affection, which you claim to value, have operated on or through you beyond the limited confines of your immediate family is a mystery."

"Having limited sympathy is not the same as having none at all. Everyone privileges his own and his relatives' survival above that of others."

The snake's forked tongue moved up and down in its open jaw at an invisible speed. "Whether or not that's true, you're exceptional insofar as power and compassion are directly correlated; the more one has of the former, the better able one is to bestow the latter. You, being all-powerful, have the potential to be all-merciful. You have chosen not to be, however, which is both convenient and beneficial to you, and which eliminates the moral advantage you might otherwise have had over me. In fact, it is safe to say that your obligation to help instead of hurt weaker animals equals or even exceeds your capacity to do so, making it the greatest mandate in the forest now that man is gone, something only a monster could ignore. And yet you think that having been born a tiger you can pursue your pleasure regardless of its cost to others."

The tiger caught no more scent of the opossum. He did not need to keep listening to the sophistry of a snake when somewhere in the vicinity Cousin and Aunt and Sister and Great-Niece and Niece and Second Cousin were either huddled together, too hungry to move or cry out, praying to the hidden sun for his return, or under the influence of a young pretender stealing what belonged to him.

As he considered where to look for them, a rustling sound to the east preceded the appearance of fifteen zebras galloping across the clearing in a westward direction, followed immediately by a herd of long-necked giraffes. The rain was falling steadier now and vast puddles formed on the ground. Then, from opposite corners of the clearing, two new sets of animals emerged—from the southeast peacocks, and from the northeast rabbits—to unite on the path trampled first by the zebras and then by the giraffes.

"Where are they going?" shouted the tiger to the snake, who had ascended to the topmost branch and was staring into the distance.

The snake didn't answer for several minutes, during which bunches of toads, rhinoceros, goats, horses, gorillas, short-haired cats, mice, beetles, and marmots filed past, until finally, with an unreadable expression, it returned to its perch on the fourth-lowest branch and said, "They are headed west."

"But why?"

Rain poured down so heavily now that the tiger felt a uniform pressure on his back. A flock of geese flew above while an assortment of chimpanzees and foxes and deer raced by. The puddles converged into an unbroken pool. Next came wolves and bears and badgers and lambs, and it was a marvel to see the peaceful—the non-murderous—lockstep of predators with their prey.

The tiger said to the snake, who still had not answered, "Is there higher ground to the west, or perhaps a fire to the east?"

"No."

"Then what did you see?"

"Earlier you said that I delight in destruction and trick noble animals such as man. I'll tell you what I saw, but first you must hear something."

The rain fell insistently and the tiger was too weary to protest.

"When Eve came here she was a child. Not biologically, but in temper and intellectual development she was little better than the clay from which Adam was formed. I lived on the ground then and ate a sparse diet of mice and other small fry, with little interest in this tree. Eve used to stand where you are now and ask herself whether she should or shouldn't eat its fruit. Her life was tiresome, she'd say, without variation or intrigue or intensity of feeling—everything she did produced the same dull note—and eating the fruit would change that. Unless it wouldn't. What if, she'd say, an unpredictable life of alternating pain and joy and mystery was as unsatisfying as the one of regular contentment and predictability she currently led? What if the afterward were different from the before in kind but not in degree? And while the prospect of death might invest life with greater meaning than it currently possessed, on the theory that something's value rises in proportion to its scarcity, it might do the opposite and fill her with a sense of life's futility."

The water level had reached the halfway point on the tiger's legs, and he decided to start walking west with the blind hope of finding his companions, who might intercede on his behalf with their new leader. There was no reason to stay here.

The snake said, "One day, after months of ignoring me, she asked what I thought she should do. Stay and suffer in a familiar manner, with an inevitable increase in boredom as time passed meaninglessly, or eat the fruit and be banished to a place and mode of being that might as easily be worse as be better, and that would come to an end? She couldn't ask Adam because he wanted nothing more than to love and admire creation; he wouldn't condone her eating the fruit of this tree because he was not dissatisfied. I told her that if that were the case, she could do no wrong that would not also be right."

The tiger's stomach now grazed the water's surface, along which a thousand raindrops ignited in tiny explosions that added to and overlapped and canceled one another out. A memory came to him of standing on an open plain during a heat wave when he was young, under a bleached white sky dirtied in the distance by specks of vultures circling over the elk he had just slain, at which time, stupefied but not yet made frantic by thirst, and for a moment on the other side of a small hill from the others, a single droplet of water had fallen on his nose. There had been no clouds or birds above him, and no rivers within sight to produce this moisture. He'd licked it away and in the fraction of relief it afforded him he'd felt his yearning for more spike to an unbearable degree, and he'd had a vision then of endless water, of a flood like the one now arising, and he'd understood that the leadership responsible for taking the pride so far from a fresh drinking supply, and which just moments before had failed to help him bring down the elk, needed to be replaced.

"Do you know what she did then?" asked the snake.

The tiger could clearly see his father's body perched that evening at the mouth of the cave where the pride was sleeping, his muscles thin and shrunken, his ears perfectly still, lost in a memory of the world as someplace new, when the cycle of rise and fall was not yet known.

"She walked away and never returned."

A strong current now ran through the water. The tiger's feet were firmly on the ground, though he couldn't say for how much longer they could stay there. The rain stripped leaves and pine needles from the trees around him and left bare branches stabbing the blackened sky. A bolt of lightning lit up the clearing in a white flash as the tiger bent down to lap up a mouthful of water, which tasted of loamy soil and bones and aloe and bark and insects and iron and sap and stone and the dust of an ended drought, diluted by tears and thickened by blood. As he drank more the tiger became thirstier.

"To the west," said the snake, now on a lower branch, "not far from here, no more than two furlongs away, is a giant ship. A gangway connects the ground and its deck, and is being used to convey up pairs of animals. Even in your condition you could reach it in time."

The tiger kept his eyes down and drank away his recent hunger and the whelps of Sister's cubs and the illusion that there would never be a young tiger half again his size. He swallowed his father's murder and the years he'd led his pride through a shrinking forest and the moment he'd known that his confidence was built on a decaying foundation. He consumed the love and hatred that had once given him vitality, and the times when his survival had been in question, and when it had been a foregone conclusion, and when it had been a matter of neither indifference nor consequence.

The snake came down to the lowest branch and extended its head to within a foot of the tiger's and said, "We could go to the boat together. I could ride on your back and navigate."

The tiger didn't look up or stop drinking. There was so much more to take in. He'd only just begun.

CONCORD

Cameron Salters hadn't always wanted to be an investment banker. In college he'd been a music major, and an emeritus professor had stopped him once and said, "Theory, technical precision, timing, notational literacy: the man who denigrates these is a fool and you must spurn him always. And yet my dear boy," the professor's arm found its way around Cameron's shoulders and his faint breath touched the student's neck, "by chance or design you were born with tremendously powerful lungs. I heard you in Dr. Lasky's class exhale for two and a half minutes without a moment's tremolo. Being so young you cannot appreciate this gift. It is beyond your powers of comprehension, but it is not beyond mine." The professor was Bavarian and mostly blind and too elderly to be a sexual threat, so Cameron accepted the praise. And had his father's health the following year not forced him to give up the French horn and study microeconomics, he might have developed his gift further and become a musician.

Instead he got an MBA, earned more than his parents, and suspected when he woke up in the morning and went to work and negotiated client annuities and came home and went to bed, that he'd made a mistake in life. On foggy nights, parked at Pier 27 on the Embarcadero, staring across the Bay at the aureole over Oakland and listening to the deep chord sidewinding of Bach's cello suites,

Cameron sometimes thought, purely hypothetically, of sealing off his garage when he got home and letting the engine run. Watching a million city lights, in a luxury sedan that made less noise idling than it did turned off, he would imagine his own requiem and consider the irony of no longer being able to play it.

Since meeting her at a mutual friend's barbecue two years earlier, Cameron had dated Janet Quinn, a junior executive consultant at the city's premier branding company. Janet's clients included top apparel, appliance, and e-commerce companies that wanted to know America's attitude toward their logos and niche appeal. Each company acted, Janet thought, like a nervous teenage boy uncertain if the girl he liked ever talked about him and unable to make a move in her direction until he was sure she'd say yes. Companies were timorous. They were confused. Which was why Janet felt more like a therapist than a consultant, someone whose job was to talk the corporate world through its neuroses to a point where launching an ad campaign was unaccompanied by fear and trembling.

Not having to work Cameron's hours, Janet still had friends who weren't coworkers, although she'd lost two of them to marriage in April and ever since had been on the lookout for replacement friends who weren't picky about movies. Not that Janet wanted to dominate the decision-making process when going to see something, but rather she didn't need a high-brow companion for whom any suggestion of going to a multiplex raised concerns about America's cultural mores. Her friends in college and immediately afterward had been like this, but she was an adult now and didn't need disappointment and unhappy endings in her entertainment. She got enough of these in the course of an average month.

Unknown to Cameron, Janet had a lover named Ryan Conlin whom everyone called Wry, because that's what he was, all the time, even when Janet was having a candid conversation with him about a client's preference for her rival's inane ad strategy over the brilliant one she'd spent a week of halogen midnights developing. Especially then. He didn't seem to care and would even mock her a little, prop himself up on the couch and make fun of what she did and cared about professionally, which may not have been running a soup kitchen for the Tenderloin's downtrodden but at least wasn't dealing black tar heroin on the corner of Mission and Sixteenth to low-profile celebrities' kids who sharked along in tinted-windowed sport utility vehicles. Which was to say that her life and priorities ought to have been kept in perspective, that in the rising tide of twenty-first century America there were always better and worse things one could be doing.

And what infuriated Janet about Wry's condescending attitude, as opposed to just hurting or humiliating her, was Wry's hypocrisy. What, after all, did he do besides temp work at a public interest law firm and study Butoh dancing with that bald contortionist Kirin Sortoga? When had he devoted even a single weekend afternoon to driving a van for Meals on Wheels or manning a phone at a suicide prevention hotline? Never, that's when. So Janet was content to let this affair play itself out while she spent more and more evenings in Café Abir, hoping to meet someone at the espresso counter who would notice her copy of *The French Lieutenant's Woman* and say, "That's funny, I was just in Lyme Regis." This hope sprang eternal.

Wry was grateful that Janet hadn't made any moves to increase their togetherness, because he took issue with sexual constancy. His issue was that he was incapable of it and had never been monogamous by choice. Generously, he gave his romantic attention to anyone who needed it and even tried to give it to people whose demand was less overt, people who thought of it simply as a passable way to spend a few hours, a may-as-well sort of gift. Provided the woman didn't do it first, Wry would end these dalliances if and when a pattern developed—like regular phone calls or questions about what he did when not with the person questioning him.

Until now. Now he felt something unusual and didn't know how to proceed in the matter of Tsitsi Mbogomi and his growing feelings for her. He felt more boyish than he had as a child and thought dizzily about their first meeting, when she'd spilled a Big Gulp soda on his sun-bleached mohair coat while standing in line to see a triple-feature Satyajit Ray retrospective at the Red Vic Movie House. He knew that they were destined for each other and had been waiting their entire lives for that bitter evening of Pacific-sprung winds and everyone in line huddling as close together as at an airport departure gate, talking about park-side sublets and digital poetry.

Tsitsi, tall and black and with microdot freckles running from cheek to cheek across her broad, flat nose, had been telling a story to her Zimbabwean friends before she sneezed, her left arm jerked slightly, and she said, "Shit!" She and her friends and Wry stared at Wry's dripping coat and the long strip of cilia smoothed down and darkened by her cola. "I'm so sorry," she said, blowing her nose into a Calamity Jane handkerchief with authentically tattered selvage.

Wry stared for a moment at his ruined coat before looking up at her indignantly for a second too long that became hey-wait-a-minute. The spiller appeared as contrite and breathed as heavily as if she'd just set off an avalanche. She made a hesitant gesture to daub the coat with the clean part of her handkerchief but instead held back, clearly afraid that by touching it she'd make it worse. Wry felt then just how inconsequential his coat was, how vainglorious he'd been to own anything sun-bleached and mohair, so he took it off and dropped it into a streetlamp-chained garbage can. In the same motion he took her hand in his, squeezed it softly, and said his full name, Ryan Hanlon Conlin. He shivered to the point where he squinted.

"I feel awful," Tsitsi said. "And that's a beautiful coat. Do you really have to throw it away? I'd be happy to pay for it to be dry cleaned."

"That old thing?" answered Wry, his arms aflame with goose bumps. "I've been wanting to get rid of it for a long time." He ignored the throat-clearing that came at his side from Lynn, the coworker with whom he had flirted for several weeks and come to the theater. Lynn, his date. Running a hand over his short magenta hair, he focused on the spiller.

But after Tsitsi didn't give her name in return for Wry's and the balance spiked in her favor and he grew frantic about how to prolong this meeting, especially given Lynn's continued *you-asshole* coughing, the line lurched forward into the theater and Wry found himself in a seat three rows and seven columns down from where Tsitsi sat between the Zimbabweans. He craned his neck in Tsitsi's direction while Lynn reminded him of how proud he'd been of his mohair coat, of how that very afternoon he'd spoken to fellow paralegal Pat Hisatsu about its inimitable blend of style and comfort. Wry absently agreed to being stupid as he tried to see around the porkpie hat of a grizzled old hipster sitting to his left and directly in his eyepath to Tsitsi. If he hadn't caught a glimpse of her exiting figure after the first movie and leapt up to overtake her in the lobby, he'd never have discovered her name or where she lived or her phone number, and he'd never have extracted her reluctant permission to call.

Despite the city's steady demand for string quartets to play at charity fundraisers, all-denominational weddings, birthday parties, career retrospectives, and funerals, Tsitsi's group, the Peony Quartet, didn't secure enough gigs to pay for their all-black performance outfits or meet their monthly rents. After promoting the group through canvassing and poster postings and arts agency affiliation, Tsitsi still had to supplement her income by working from six in the morning to three in the afternoon, Monday through Thursday, at Specialty's Bakery in the Financial District. Although bored and depressed by the work, she'd become an expert at anything to do with lemon poppyseed, and her potato cheddar muffins were considered nonpareil by people who'd had them everywhere. Customers and coworkers approached her about catering their get-togethers. She would accept on the condition that they let her quartet provide the music. "A quartet," they'd say deliberately. "That's an interesting idea, except that my friends are more into electro-blues." Or big band swing. Or country hip hop klezmer waltzes. So Tsitsi would decline the catering job and feel prematurely old for her twenty-five years, discouraged that classical music was such an untenable pursuit outside of graduate school or nepotistic urban orchestras. She'd begun to take seriously the fear that she was practicing a dead art.

One day, when three suited men entered Specialty's during the pre-lunch lull, Tsitsi was bent down behind the display counter, rearranging the muffin tray in a sweet to savory direction so that it progressed from blueberry to wheat germ. Standing up and seeing the men study the menu, she looked around for her coworkers and saw none who could take their order while she went to the bathroom.

She squirmed impatiently. One of the men was tall, wore a navy blue pinstripe suit, and had thinning hair grown long for one last glory run. His four-day beard was patchy and sculpted to reinforce his slight jawline. Another, similarly dressed but in gray, was smaller and hairier, with two diamond earrings and a stud in his tragus. The third was of average height and build, and he had, while regarding the pastries, the most intense look of concentration Tsitsi had ever seen on a customer, as though he were examining children at an adoption center rather than choosing between strawberry and plain cheese Danishes. Finally he ordered a croissant and cup of coffee with an added espresso shot.

Tsitsi assembled the man's order and was counting out his change when she heard him whistle Henryk Mikolaj Górecki's "Arioso." She almost dropped a handful of shiny new dimes. Giving him a shriveling receipt and a shy smile, she said, "Quasi una fantasia."

"*Si*," he said, evidently surprised, and then he took the coffee cup by its cardboard, heat-diffusing handle and withdrew to an island counter on which was a row of thermoses.

"The middle one's half and half," Tsitsi called out, seeing him hesitate. "The label rubbed off and I haven't replaced it yet."

"Thanks." He topped up his coffee with cream and waited for his friends to join him.

The next day Tsitsi was in the kitchen letting 144 snickerdoodles cool when Gypsy Kate opened the door to tell her that some guy was looking for her out front.

"What does he want?" Tsitsi asked, prying up the cookies from a nonstick baking pan the size of a truck windshield.

"What does every guy want?" Gypsy Kate said.

"Are you serious?"

"Who knows?"

After sliding the cookies onto four serving plates, Tsitsi went out to the front and saw the Górecki man. She retied her apron and stepped aside for a deliverywoman pushing a dolly loaded with pasteurized fruit juices. The plangent whistle of an espresso machine's steaming lever. The rattle of soup lids. A wrong-number phone call.

"Are you looking for me?" she asked, brushing tight black curls out of her eyes and feeling sweaty and gross, like she should not see anyone today except for the flour wholesaler.

"Yeah." The man's short brown hair, previously sprayed into an everyman side-part, stuck out in ladyfinger clumps. Wearing a misbuttoned argyle sweater and wrinkled chinos, he had bruise-colored bags under his eyes and the sallow complexion of a scurvy victim. He swayed a little on his feet between the order counter and the condiment island. "My name is Cameron Salters," he said, "and I got coffee from you yesterday."

"I remember."

"It's probably not your fault, but I think there was something wrong with the cream in this, um…" He weakly tapped a big round gray thing with a sort of nozzle dispenser at the top.

"Thermos."

"Right." He smiled thankfully. "Thermos. I drank it and threw up all night. Then I threw up all morning. The worst is probably over but the point is that I think the cream is what made me sick. It tasted funny."

Tsitsi walked to the island, unscrewed the top of the middle thermos, and smelled the fatty cream swishing thickly inside. She stared at the collagen film left on the curved steel wall when the liquid settled, and said, "I'm sorry about that. I'd be happy to give you some complimentary coupons if you want, or you could talk to the manager to lodge a formal complaint."

Cameron shook his head. "That's okay. I just wanted to let you know so that no one else gets sick."

"Definitely," Tsitsi said. "Sometimes we get in a rush and forget to look at carton dates when we're refilling the thermoses, but usually our dairy products are fresh enough to not worry. We get them from over there." She pointed to the door and the culture clash of a hundred people passing by outside.

"From where?"

"From Berkeley."

"Oh," Cameron said. "Well, all right. Thanks."

He left and Tsitsi sighed. Seemed like a nice guy who might have been more receptive to hiring the Peony Quartet than most people she met. Certainly complained in a considerate way. As recently as Monday, a stooped, caftan-hooded woman set aside a half hour of her day to complain to Tsitsi for giving her a sandwich with cilantro. Although the sandwich's menu description listed cilantro, the woman pointed to faint red spots on her hand that she claimed were the beginning of "a terrible allergic ravishing," and that with an ingredient as hateful as cilantro, a dozen bolded warnings were the least a bakery could provide. Not to be placated by Tsitsi's offer of complimentary coupons, the woman left with the threat-promise never to return.

Two days after Cameron came in sick, when Tsitsi had essentially forgotten him and was counting money from the closed express line till, he came back and ordered a croissant and espresso-laced coffee from Gypsy Kate. It was 11:17 a.m., and although the night crew traditionally refilled the bulk bins of coffee beans at the end of the day, Tsitsi thought the bins looked low.

"You whistle very well," she said when standing next to Cameron and struggling to open a fifty-pound canvas bag of Ethiopian dark roast. The knotted string at the bag's opening was in a hopeless skein.

"Do you need help with that?" he asked.

"I've got it." But she didn't have it and so turned her attention to straightening the nearby shelves of for-sale travel mugs. "Really, you got every note of Górecki right. That's amazing."

Cameron stirred his coffee. "I used to play the cornet in my high school marching band."

"Really? And you got Górecki from that?"

"In college I played the French horn. I started as a music major and wanted to go to Juilliard and then set up a private tutoring practice in Sebastopol. I was going to build a little army of horn players."

The mugs were perfect, but Tsitsi kept eyeballing them. "That didn't happen?"

"My dad had a stroke when I was a sophomore, and afterward I had to pay my own way through college, so I became an economics major."

"I'm sorry."

"I think about going back to it sometimes." He fitted a flimsy lid on his to-go coffee cup and took a sip, turning to face the door. "I'd be terrible, though. It's been a long time since I played regularly."

Tsitsi felt the pinpricks of something that she tried to eliminate by thinking about her baking schedule for that afternoon, hoping to control the sensation in the same way that imagining warmth can sometimes overcome feeling cold. She watched Cameron leave and thought very, very hard about the muffins she'd later make.

Janet had never known jealousy because she'd never been in a have-hold relationship with someone whose fidelity was worth worrying about.

"I'd encourage him to have an affair," she told Barb, her manicurist, "except that it takes him so long to get comfortable enough for sex that most women would get bored and give up. After the first time we kissed—this was on our third date—he looked away all ashamed and said he was sorry for rushing things, that we were basically strangers and how would I think of him now other than 'that wolf' or something, and what could he do to make amends? I said, 'I was the one who kissed you.' But then he went on about how he appreciates my taking the blame but that he knows he's responsible because he hasn't thought of anything but kissing me from the moment we met." Janet stared at the tiny fake pearls that Barb lacquered onto her nails. "And what's weird is that at first I was mad at him for being such a dumb pig and implying that I don't have sexual urges or am too ladylike to instigate a kiss, and I was about to say fuck this, I don't need a guy who in some ways is attractive and likeable but who for all I know four dates later is impotent or gay or sworn to chastity. But then just as I opened my mouth it was like someone played harp scales and I thought that this was the sweetest moment I'd ever experienced, a guy saying that all he's wanted to do for the past three dates is kiss me, but has restrained himself on account of Old World decorum. And he's even rewritten events in his head to imagine that he had finally snapped and kissed me because he couldn't control himself any longer! I thought, *this is stupendously romantic*, and I felt a flutter in my chest and everywhere else. It was only later that I realized he *had not* in reality been unable to control himself any longer, and that if I hadn't done anything he wouldn't have, either, and that as far as bed tricks went he probably had the self-restraint to resist them until we were both dead."

Barb nodded and said the same thing had happened to her once, but when she looked at her watch she saw that it was the end of Janet's half-hour appointment, so she folded up her kit and told Janet not to put her hands in her pockets for at least an hour.

"As if I didn't know that," Janet thought, and overturned her purse for a five-dollar tip in coins.

The San Francisco Ballet was performing *Giselle*. Janet had seen it at least once when she was a child and would have declined Cameron's invitation if he hadn't been so excited on the phone about getting the last two available seats, and *with the world-famous Finnish conductor Lasse Lindstrom at the orchestra's helm*. Well, quick rush hurry, get me smelling salts. A coworker of Cameron's had come down with bronchitis that morning and given him two seats in balcony section G with the caveat that they might be obstructed viewing behind support columns. There was nothing "might" about it. Janet's nose practically nuzzled marble as she refused Cameron's offers of the binoculars, thinking that it was for boring times like this that she should develop a good meditation practice—either concentrating on her chakra points or on a distant light bulb or on her respiration. She needed a clock-accelerating technique to fix delayed buses, hair drying, and nights at the ballet.

When it ended Janet gave a hippopotamus yawn and wiped the sleep from her eyes. Slow-building applause in the auditorium became as thick as a monsoon, mist sprinkle rain downpour deluge downpour rain sprinkle mist. Janet and Cameron rose and held hands while walking up the baby steps of section G, away from their sightless seats. The hand was so she didn't lose him, not because she loved him. No, the no-love thought coursed through her like a rush of anxiety; she absolutely didn't love this man whose hand now slipped out of hers to position his binoculars perfectly in the mold of a velveteen carrying case. He fell back but she kept going. First one bejeweled gentleman separated them on the andante stampede out, then another. When Janet reached the elevator going down, she couldn't see Cameron at all in the mass of lined foreheads and low necklines. The doors parted and a woman standing inside with powerfully straight gray hair raised her eyebrows questioningly. Janet stepped in alone and felt her heart go up.

Wry's attempts to woo Tsitsi hit a snag. Specifically, she ignored his six most recent phone calls and sent only one response to his emails: "It was nice to see you last week, and I hope you don't regret the coat too much. Take care, Tsitsi." It didn't brim with innuendo. He came to the conclusion that after their single date, on which they'd eaten at the Stinking Rose, been to four different bars, and wound up having nothing to say to one another at the Golden Gate Bridge visitor center after his disastrously long monologue on Butoh dancing and the charismatic power of Kirin Sortoga, she was uninterested in him and wished to be left alone. Yet how could he know that Tsitsi wasn't mistakenly turning her back on lifelong happiness? How could he in good conscience let it go without one final effort?

With the Yuletide season approaching, Wry persuaded the law office where he worked, Morrison & Foerster, to hire the Peony Quartet for its holiday party. The theme was Louis XIV France, so Tsitsi's group could do an evening of Baroque standards. Securing her this gig, he hoped, would demonstrate his good faith in their relationship and make her beholden to him so that he could someday make an honest woman of her and an honest man of himself.

With the ready commitment of the other Peonies and an acceptance tendered, Tsitsi talked about the party performance to Cameron the next time he was at Specialty's, and in a roundabout manner invited him to come if he didn't have anything else to do that night and didn't mind making small talk with some low-powered attorneys who, at least, had placed a huge hors d'oeuvres order with her.

"Does your girlfriend like classical music?" she asked him while wiping off a few clumps of brown sugar from the counter, hoping he'd laugh off the notion of his having a girlfriend and say with unmistakable gravitas that while he hadn't found her yet, he thought he was getting close.

Instead he shook his head and said, "She'll tolerate it, but she's more into contemporary pop music. You know, the Forgive-Me-Nots and Entropy Now."

Tsitsi said, "I don't know them."

"Me neither," he said.

She wiped the spot where once there'd been a few sugar granules but which now was clean enough to reflect objects placed on it, and she suggested that he bring his girlfriend anyway, that maybe she could arrange for some Enemy Now to be played during the intermission.

"All right," he said, ruffling the part out of his hair and picking up his coffee. "I'd love to come. I mean, we'd love to come."

Tsitsi said nothing and fought a lump at the back of her throat that made her breathing catch on something unlocatable as she watched Cameron leaving and knew that as surely as she was born alone, she would die alone.

The city's SoMa district was all gala as limos and box cabs released festive digerati and their significant others into its space shuttle warehouses and lantern-lit clubs. Billboards shone down like so many scenes from heaven. Although normally tolerant of the city's jobless people, SoMa wasn't happy this evening about its street corners, where they were standing around with brown paper bags and pocketsful of fingers, talking about the flotsam they'd picked up during the day and stored in whichever dumpster they called home. Hence the police leaf-blowing derelicts to less photographed alleyways and arresting more than a night's quota of graffiti artists and leather exhibitionists. Who wanted to have their holiday party besmirched by a lot of *les misérables* who couldn't sing or dance or disappear in the billowy smoke of a dry ice machine?

Cameron and Janet found a tight parking spot on tenth and Howard so close to where they were going that they'd be able talk about their good parking karma for a week. When they stepped out of the car, a guy stumbled over from a chain-link fence to describe his night watchman services, saying that for a mere three dollars he'd protect their car until dawn, and couldn't they help him out on account of times was hard? Before he could finish, two officers arrived to detain him and nod apologetically at Cameron and Janet, who would be three dollars richer and a veil of security lighter, and who watched as the man yelled something incomprehensible while struggling to walk fast enough for the rangy-limbed officers gamboling back to their squad car.

At the Crumbling Empire, a double-decker bar on Ninth St. rented for the evening's celebration by Morrison & Foerster, the Peony Quartet unfolded their chairs and screwed together music stands. From next door, a bass line infiltrated the walls. Tsitsi suggested that she and her fellow musicians hook up their instruments to the amplifiers they'd brought, that otherwise it'd be impossible to compete with the cavernous thumps.

While she looked for an electrical outlet near enough to the performance stage for all four amps to reach, Wry, wearing a wig of six-inch-high white curls, crushed velvet knee-length pants, white stockings, and an all-frills hemp shirt, approached her.

"Hey, Tsitsi," he said, "you look great. Very professional."

"Thanks," Tsitsi replied, her conservative black dress cloaking her body in the dark. "And you look very authentic."

"It's the dauphin in me."

Tsitsi smiled and shook Wry's hand as though meeting him for the first time, then got back to squinting at the wall's floor line and pushing back tables to get a better view. Giving up, she turned around and saw Wry still standing there, now almost too close for comfort. "I'm looking for electrical outlets," she said.

"Absolutely," answered Wry, steeling himself for what he needed to say. But she was already turning away and had a foot on the steps leading up to the stage, so he shouted quickly, "Hey! I was wondering, because I know you're only supposed to play until midnight, if you'd be into grabbing a drink later?"

Tsitsi took her foot off the stair and faced him. "I'm, well," she began, her eyes on Wry's plumage, not rising to meet his, because this was a difficult moment that she knew had been coming and regretted not having prepared for. "I think you're a really nice guy," she said in a downward declension, as if instead of complimenting him she was telling him he had stomach cancer. She knew that this was the wrong tone considering her neutral-to-good thoughts about him, her belief that he was perfectly smart and attractive albeit self-absorbed to a degree that was unattractive to her. She said, significantly, "Do you know what I mean?"

Wry was not an idiot, but he wished he was now in this wretched moment. He'd secured this performance for her and nothing for himself. On the surface it was nothing worse than a hundred other non-affairs in which someone had been uninterested in him, but this drilled below surfaces and struck a real sentiment rather than the standard there's-always-plenty-more attitude that had propelled him through so many years without experiencing heartbreak. He felt like a fool in these clothes, in this position, in this tale. He had become the wrong person.

All around, lawyers, secretaries, and paralegals were walking uncertainly in their aristocratic outfits, bumping into chairs as they trailed after the plates of hors d'oeuvres. Accustomed to dealing with each other solely in terms of business, they weren't sure how loudly to laugh at the spectacle of each other's outfits, or how boisterous to make their toasts, or how candid to be about cases officially off-limits to outside conversations. So when Cameron and Janet walked in and quietly became aware that they were the only people who didn't look personally opposed to *liberté*, *fraternité* and *egalité*, their discomfort wasn't out of place.

"Who are these people, again?" Janet asked as they ordered drinks at the bar. A woman with blood-red cheeks and an overemphasized mole painted on her upper lip stepped between them and grabbed two pre-poured white wines. Janet gave her a do-you-mind look, which the woman disregarded before walking away. Janet immediately forgot her annoyance when she saw Wry, topping her list of people she didn't expect or want to see this evening, take the woman's place and stand there for a moment contemplating the liquor shelf.

"Wry?" Janet said.

"Janet?" Wry said.

"You two know each other?" asked Cameron, flipping his pointer finger between them.

Tsitsi joined them at the wet bar, having come to ask if there was an extension cord lying around behind it. She'd held out, in the wee small hours of her subconscious, for the possibility that Cameron and this woman would break up before tonight or that the girlfriend would move away or have a regrettable accident. Tsitsi had fed herself these dream candies and now had to face an empty box.

"Hi, Cameron," she said. "Thanks for coming. We're about to begin, just as soon as I can get our instruments plugged in. Do you know Ryan?"

"We were about to meet," Cameron said. "He knows my friend Janet. Janet, this is Tsitsi."

A round robin of hi's. Some mortification. Some guilt. Some innocence. Some intuition of what was really going on, some repression thereof. The cool, agony-soothing effect of a respectably aged and drier-than-cork Cabernet Sauvignon. An order for Bombay Sapphire and tonic upgraded to a triple. The erratic thud of next door's music. And some of us were meant to find that one person, that fabled corollary who'd make the inadequacy we feel vanish due to the profusion that would be us, but there was to be no guarantee that the timing would be right or the foreknowledge reciprocated or the luck ours to do anything about it. What a piece of work is woman, the future of man.

Beginning with a selection from Couperin's *Les Nations*, the Peony Quartet worked its way through an hour of Baroque quadrilles that endowed the Morrison & Foerster employees with a delicate lightness of step on the dance floor. Couples improvised elaborate pavanes that segued into galliards and arced into circular branles that moved into progressive longways whenever people got excited enough to collectivize their pleasure. Tsitsi glanced up from her score and was overwhelmed by the grace of her audience. Her strings had never felt so pliant nor her fingerboard so steady. The notes she played bound her, one by one, to the moving bodies on the floor below, like a miracle that everyone's witnessed and that seems to be the most natural of phenomena. Like water into wine, like forty loaves.

Except that for Cameron it was more akin to the burning bush; he was transfixed in his seat at an empty booth next to an unplugged jukebox, watching Tsitsi's fingers slide and bend and stop firm while her bow seesawed up and down and side to side. He had sat alone since Janet excused herself to go to the bathroom and on her way back stopped to talk to Ryan near the side exit. An untouched drink in front of Cameron slowly leaked condensation down its sides, flooding an illegible coaster. He folded his hands and entered the rapture, at last, of knowing what had to be done.

In the rubicund glow of the Crumbling Empire's exit sign, Janet and Wry figured it out. The idea that they could have an affair dissociated from mutual respect and efforts at consistency and the smallest, most rudimentary attentions paid to one another's true selves, whatever those were, struck them now as absurd. Wry knew that he couldn't play Russian roulette forever, that it must end badly. "Did you know that once I stopped by your apartment to pick up a coat I'd left there, and I heard spanking and giggling from inside?" Janet asked. "I could have been alone," Wry said. And they laughed. And they said goodbye. And they both knew that they were better off alone and free to devote themselves to something real, when and if it at last came. One could be a peripheral figure in one's own life for only so long.

"Cameron," Janet said, as she slid onto the booth's puffy vinyl seat opposite him.

Cameron came to attention and looked at her.

"I should tell you something but not for the reason you're going to think at first."

"Okay."

"You know that guy you met earlier, Ryan?"

"I do."

"I've been having an affair with him for the past year. Not regular, like twice a week, but enough so that I have to tell you to be honest."

"I see."

"I'm not just trying to clear my conscience here. It's more that I think you and I have come to a crossroads. And the only solution I see us finding is to split up. There's a better way to say this but I don't know how to do it."

Cameron was silent for a long time. "You're right," he said. "I was actually going to tell you that I'm leaving San Francisco."

"You are?"

"I'm moving to Sebastopol."

"When did you decide this?"

"I've been meaning to do it forever."

"So there's no better time than the present," Janet said.

"It's all we ever have."

The Peony Quartet played long after its prearranged midnight finish, and at 2 a.m., when Tsitsi had packed up her things and drunk a congratulatory beer with the other quartet members, she was very tired and very committed to getting home and then very startled to find a man she'd once mistaken as average standing alone outside the doorway to the Crumbling Empire. The bassline from next door thumped its last, and with a great intake of breath Cameron stepped forward to place his hand over hers for a second that was no more an instant than it was an eternity, and with twining fingers that would grow stronger over subsequent years of trumpeting and violining and snickerdoodling and handymanning, they touched until that touch became a kiss and that kiss became a declaration, for here and now, of two people's escape, however narrow, from the din of silence.

STARGAZING

Dee Anderson threw the best spa parties around. Her 1920s Victorian home, as dark and promising as an avocado, was set far enough back from the road near Sequoia Park that Jill could lean back in the fiberglass spa whose hydrojets massaged the backs of her legs and soles of her feet and wonder how much extraterrestrial life was up there, no streetlight glare dimming the night sky. And there'd always be a few men or women wondering with her about the civilizations on Eldobon or Xerzizody or wherever.

Jill would look around the cedar deck with the spa quietly burbling, the house on one side and lawn on the other, and think, "This is going to end too fast." Over by the all-night barbecue, there'd be Dan Stixon, Fortuna mayor, flirting with a couple from McKinleyville who belonged to the Humboldt Artists Guild with Dee. And beneath the portico leading into the house would be five nude men and women comparing skin flaws, the scars and birthmarks and fungi that didn't respond to over-the-counter topical creams, getting ready to go to the master bedroom. And cool jazz on the hi-fi, or spaghetti western overtures, lending the sharp night air the feeling of deep remoteness.

Not that it mattered what the soundtrack was to Jill's spa night, to a break from Monday-to-Friday, to her thoughts about space and the final frontier. Dee on her left, Milo on her right, fingers and toes finding other fingers and toes, for a start. A plate of vegetable shish kebabs on the glass end table by her left elbow, a dog rubbing its boner on the sack of lawn fertilizer next to the rake.

She thought, she thought that maybe aliens were advanced creatures who had rigged their society with nutrient pills and automated labor and static government, so that nobody was left wanting or dissatisfied or angry or malcontent. She thought maybe the inhabitants of Eldobon had gotten rid of strife and so wouldn't bother seeking out other worlds, like hers for instance, being so satisfied. Because work was a four-letter word and they didn't need it. Because things were easy for them and growth a redundancy. And she started to get pissed off, because she didn't have it that easy and didn't think others should either, no matter how many light years away they were, because suffering led to wisdom, and comfort was anathema to compassion, and smug aliens, by thinking they had nothing more to learn, might as well be dead.

"Those fuckers," she said, refusing a glass of the sickly sweet Merlot that Dee had been pouring all night, removing her finger from someone's vagina, standing up and feeling lightheaded. She had to get home. What was the point of this orgy? How could they all stand around like they weren't being judged?

Dee asked what had gotten into her, and Jill asked if the world was just a pleasuredome to her.

"What?" Dee said.

"Forget it," Jill said, and grabbed her sandals and blouse, pulled on her tan corduroys, and got in her car and drove past Sequoia Park and signaled right at the stop sign without seeing the car to her left.

But it was okay, because for a long time she'd been falling and the air had been whistling past her at 9.7 meters per second squared, and she'd seen the world getting lost up there.

JANE SAYS

People say what a tragedy when you're thirteen and selling it on the street. They say what kind of parents would let that happen and what kind of police force doesn't stop it and what hope is there for him now. Your life they all agree is going to spiral down down down into some viscid cesspool where to drown would be a blessing. But they haven't personally met any of the thirteen-year-olds working the trade—not in the daytime anyway—and they owe too much to their imagination and news and movies and books, which are all more or less the same thing.

I say this because I used to be one of those thirteen-year-olds, the latest supposed lost boy of the latest lost generation, and my companions were also thirteen or fourteen or on occasion fifteen. For years I stood on street corners with Petey and Vishnu and Hirotaka talking about the night before's janes until a station wagon rolled up and its window rolled down and the lady behind the wheel took off her sunglasses to give one of us the finger call.

Most just wanted the usual young heat and hormones, but some were sick sad deviants who made you wonder even though you were the prostitute what had happened to them. It was the pitiable pitying the pitiful. One jane for example took me to her house in the Heights and instead of having me dress like an altar boy for a taboo communion, paid me to study math in her kitchen while she filed her taxes online. Another drove me to and from junior league soccer practice in the suburbs every afternoon for a week. A third had me demand sugared cereal in a supermarket aisle while she refused to let me poison myself until a cashier told us we'd have to quiet down or leave the store, whereupon she cried and held me tightly and said okay, just this once, I could have it.

Because life is hard.

Consider my last night working. I was standing in front of a twenty-four-hour juice bar, Petey and Vishnu just back from a race-riot orgy put together by some creaky hotel heiress, when a jane flashed her brights from across the street. P and V were too tired to jump so I went over and got in and was told to get comfortable for a drive, and an hour later we were way out in the countryside, passing elk-crossing signs and blackened ponds and houses with names.

We stopped at a little unlit boarded-up gas station. I figured we were there to role-play—the rustic young gas attendant meets the randy old socialite—and I asked if she had a uniform for me, but she didn't answer. Five minutes later I told her we were on the clock and she said, "I'm going to give you all my money. And my house. And my car." I asked what she was talking about. "You deserve it after what you've been through. And I've written a note absolving you of all responsibility, so no one will suspect foul play." I said, *Foul play?* "My family has been expecting this a long time." I told her she was scaring me. "Yes, it's scary, but you'd know that better than anyone. People use you and don't see you for who you really are, and it's that way with all of us." I said, just to say something, that it didn't matter if no one saw me for who I really was. "Yes it does. It's necessary for us to exist. If no one sees us we're not there." She asked how I spelled my name and then wrote it on a check and on the car title and on a house deed. Handing me the sheaf of papers, she opened her door and disappeared into the shadows.

I sat there for a minute as the night air got colder and damper. It was very quiet. I unbuckled my seatbelt and stepped outside. "Lady!" I yelled. "Hey!" I went in the direction she'd gone, and behind the gas station I entered a solid darkness, where I tripped on a clanging object and stopped and listened and stared but heard and saw nothing. I had a feeling, though, that she was just ahead and that if she made a sound even accidentally I would be able to locate her. "Lady," I said, "I don't know how to drive. You can't leave me out here like this." The silence and blackness were loud and blinding. "You've got to take me back to the city." I felt detached from my body. "Lady?" There was a sharp crack, like a branch breaking right next to me.

"Lady?" I said, almost in a whisper, as though speaking softly would close the space between us, as though about existence she'd been wrong.

HUMPHREY DEMPSEY

Lord Underwood pincered the small doctor's arm. "If the King imagines that the people will stand for Lord Dempsey to be slandered—or worse, allowed to die—he has been breathing the court's febrile air for too long."

The doctor bowed at the neck and turned to leave, but Lord Underwood held him fast.

"Do not repeat a word of what you just told me to anyone, or your medical career, to start with, will come to an abrupt end."

The doctor returned to the operating tent. Lord Underwood pressed his ear to the blue- and yellow-striped door flap and heard a chiseled sound like that of masons aligning stones on a prison wall. Behind him, a dozen plumes of black smoke tunneled into the blue sky from the Tournament events that had ended an hour before. On the narrow foxglove-lined road a dozen yards away, sections of the homebound crowd staggered past, clanging tin cups and singling off to purge and relieve themselves.

This should not have happened. If Lord Underwood had drunk less ale—if he hadn't felt so festive in light of the Aqueduct Plan's upcoming passage—he would have had the wit to run down after his friend and convey him north before the King's men could bring him to this pretend hospital. Even now he had to hold his head still to stop it from spinning off into the dark.

"Are you all right, your Lordship?" asked a page with glowing red cheeks, squatting beside his master's phaeton with a misshapen orange mutt leashed to his ankle.

Lord Underwood closed his eyes, opened them, and then marched into the tent. "Out!" he yelled to the men huddling around a supine figure. "Everyone! Leave us!"

In the dark interior, six gray-cloaked men tucked their metal instruments and cloth bandage spindles into hemp sacks and filed through the door flap. An apothecary sat on a tree stump in the corner stirring his pestle and mortar with childlike absorption, deaf to the evacuation, until Lord Underwood loomed over him.

When at last they were alone, Lord Dempsey, on a bed of tightly woven hay bales with a thin white sheet covering his body, his miasmic breath coming in labored gasps, whispered, "They say it's the end."

Lord Underwood stood still for a moment before carrying a stool across the room to sit with his elbows bowed out and his hands on his knees. "Then it must be the beginning! These tyros wouldn't know a fracture from a sprain if they were sober."

"They are the King's own physicians."

"And when did the King last enjoy a day's health? We'll get you north immediately, into the care of competent surgeons. Eltherington has gone for your carriage and dispatched a request for diplomatic immunity."

Lord Dempsey's eyes rolled to the left. "This is my time. I accept it."

"In the North—"

"I do not want to die en route to a foreign country, so let us use what hours remain to discuss strategy for the Aqueduct Plan vote. I think that Eltherington ought to secure the quorum while you canvass the Danforth faction. Give them constabulary rights to my Ladbroke estate if they ask for them."

"We'll talk about this after you've gotten proper medical care."

"I tell you I'm not going anywhere."

Lord Underwood leaned over and said quietly, "What if your fall was not an accident?"

Lord Dempsey stared at the ceiling.

"Terryton, disguised as a vendor, was seen hurrying away from your box."

"I felt no hands on my back."

"The King's assassins, unlike his physicians, are skilled at what they do. Eltherington saw him, though, as did Paley and Johnston."

The patient weakly scratched his leg and coughed, a low rasping sound, as of pumice scraping across a knife. "The King would never harm me."

"Dempsey, think about the currents of self-interest gathering strength as a result of your reforms. If passed, the Aqueduct Plan will cost the royal treasury one hundred thousand ducats, and with the expense of your Gendarme Deed and Grain Dispensation Act already in effect, as well as the reduced revenue from the Landowner Retribution, the King stands to lose a quarter million ducats from your actions in the next six months alone. How long did you think his personal regard for you would outweigh his pecuniary concerns?"

"A quarter million ducats is nothing to the King."

"It is everything when he is preparing for war with the North."

"All the more reason I cannot go there for medical treatment. It would be treason."

"Only against a man who wants you dead." Lord Underwood looked at a tray on the ground covered with glass containers of rust-red powder, brackish blue liquid, dried reptile limbs, and shredded green leaves. "Do you know what the doctor told me just now, outside?"

Lord Dempsey didn't answer but looked at his friend attentively. Lord Underwood slowly repeated the doctor's report. After a moment's silence, the gallop and creak of a four-horse carriage was heard coming to a stop outside the tent. They looked over at the door flap, along the center of which a vertical line of late afternoon light burned from floor to ceiling, kindling dust motes into floating sparks of white fire. "Without you to defend yourself, that gross slander will be used—if not by the King, then by his allies in the House of Lords—to undermine your reforms. For the sake of the people, you must go north and then return in full strength."

"I have sworn fealty to the Crown and promised to protect it against all aggressors, not become one myself."

"The crown is the titular head of the people, and it is to them that you owe allegiance, not to a man whose greed stands in opposition to their good."

There was a loud whinnying of horses and the light through the door flap disappeared. Lord Dempsey coughed again but barely made a sound. "If I go north, the King must know in advance that my devotion to him is inviolable, that I go only for medical reasons."

"Unless that is a stratagem, I recommend sending no word."

"It is the sole condition on which I will go."

Lord Underwood folded his hands and smiled.

At this time, the million people who lived in the kingdom were unevenly divided between the city and three dozen outlying villages and farms. A four-year drought was ongoing that, combined with the recent diversion to the kingdom's western neighbor of two rivers that originated in the North, had caused crops to fail and farmers and merchants to descend on the city to demand tax relief and grain subsidies from the royal storehouses. In answer the King had distributed five hundred pounds of bread a day to heads of household, which was insufficient to meet the people's need, and street riots broke out, necessitating, for a time, martial law, which turned the public's affection from the King to those members of the House of Lords, like Lord Dempsey, who were vigorously passing relief legislation and curbing police power. In consequence, the King, alarmed by this shift and advised by elderly military generals who had for decades served under his bellicose father, drew up plans to attack the Northern kingdom and restore the rivers to their prior course. A combination of hope and dread filled the people, whose need for water did not erase their memory of the last war, fought against the South, in which the kingdom had suffered a terrible defeat and tens of thousands of men had been killed or maimed or sold into slavery.

During that earlier conflict, as children, Lord Humphrey Dempsey and the King, then called Master Humphrey and Prince Albert, had studied under the same tutor, the brilliant eunuch Mr. Dodd, and for many years afterward had shared women and horses and country estates, dedicated verse to each other, and enjoyed a fraternal intimacy that was a pleasure for all to behold. But after the King married and Lord Dempsey took his father's seat in the House of Lords—by which time the war with the South was long lost—they only saw each other at the biannual Fontainbleu Tournament, a three-day jubilee of acrobatics and jousting and archery, with wild game banquets and ale-drinking contests and gypsy burlesques, until the drought made such extravagances impossible and the two friends no longer met socially.

When this year the King scheduled a reduced-scale Tournament in a bid to regain popular support, paying for it with his own money, he'd not anticipated a quarter of the misfortunes that would occur: five knights dead from javelin wounds, three spectators struck by stray arrows, a fire that consumed eight valuable silk tents, and a snake wrestler suffocated in the embrace of a Moroccan anaconda. None of these, however, compared to Lord Dempsey's accident, news of which spread quickly and mournfully throughout the kingdom.

Later that evening, the King, walking with his attendants down the city's dark and empty alleys and side streets, unclasped his purple oration robe and threw it at a runner, who handed him an ermine coat in return. The crescent moon hung above them like a scythe.

"You are sure he has gone north," said the King in a tight vibrato.

"A scout spotted his train, including the carriages of Lords Underwood and Eltherington, on the highway three hours ago," said Caldwell, the King's domestic consultant, holding a damp sheet of paper. "We have a copy of his note requesting diplomatic immunity from the Northern king."

The King read it and sped up his pace. "Send an envoy to retrieve him before he crosses the border."

"I'm afraid—"

"If my doctors can't cure him, we'll find others who can."

"It's too late for that," said Stanton, another consultant. "Not only will Dempsey already have reached the North by now, but he likely thinks that you ordered his death. You have no choice but to charge him, Underwood, and Eltherington with plotting against the state and have them executed upon their return."

The King stopped and his entourage eddied around him. "Why would he think I ordered his death?"

"Because Terryton's disguise came apart as he was leaving Dempsey's box on the wall."

"And what was that butcher doing near his box?"

"He thought you wanted him dead."

"I don't understand."

"He believed that you would be pleased with a solution to the Aqueduct Plan problem. Had we known beforehand, we would have stopped him."

The King began walking again, with a clipped gait, and his jaundiced face turned a dark crimson in the moonlight as his party entered the lane where his mistress lived. "Have Terryton flayed in a public ceremony tomorrow, and when he is thoroughly dead, collect his family and do worse to them. By Tuesday morning, I want every mongrel infected with Terryton blood to have died in a drawn-out spectacle. At the same time, put all of my physicians to death. Dempsey, if he lives, will see that I had nothing to do with his accident."

The party came to the door of a squat stone building whose limestone frontispiece, surrounded by a lacework of tendriled moss, glowed luminous pearl. A bull lowed from a distant field and for answer was met by the deliberate ringing of two cow bells moving toward him.

"I suspect," said Caldwell, "that Dempsey would interpret such a move as an effort to cover your involvement, and that Underwood has already urged him to lead an uprising against you when he recovers."

"Against all of us," said Stanton.

"It would be best to reward Terryton for trying to rid the kingdom of a traitor. Dress up his blunder in the robes of heroism."

The King spat on his hands and combed down his hair over its recessions. "I will not have my oldest friend killed because of a stupid misunderstanding."

"Then your blood and that of all your relatives will flow with Terryton's through the kingdom's gutters."

"Or perhaps its new aqueducts," said Caldwell.

"No," said the King, "I will talk to Dempsey when he returns, and reason shall prevail."

"Sire," said a cloaked figure at the periphery of the crowd, "I humbly request the opportunity to speak with you."

The King, his hand raised to knock on the door, turned and said, "Is that Pimlico? Were you not among the doctors who attended Dempsey today?"

"Yes, sire."

"Guards, arrest him."

"If you please, sire, I would like to explain what happened."

"Incompetence has no excuse."

Pimlico stepped forward and said, "Lord Dempsey is not what he has long purported to be."

"Take him away."

The small doctor continued nervously. "He is, I'm afraid, against reason, against nature, not in fact a man."

"I won't repeat myself!"

"Sire, I beg your patience and magnanimity, but Lord Dempsey is an egg."

In the North, Lords Eltherington and Underwood were installed in the castle's guest wing, a corniced seven-chambered suite with running water and thick downy beds. Their servants enjoyed private adjoining quarters. The evening's entertainment, a dogfight between two Alsatians followed by a theatrical in which a man and woman, performed by two identical-looking pubescent boys with flaxen gold hair, each arranged for the other's murder after hearing false rumors of infidelity, preceded a banquet meal at which the bravery and wisdom of the visiting lords were solemnly praised by their Northern counterparts.

While this went on, and late into the next morning, a team of doctors operated on Lord Dempsey; upon finishing, they confined him to bed for a week and said that he was to be very careful, that the slightest physical injury would undo their work and likely lead to his death. Thereafter in his recovery room, Lord Dempsey, too weak to move, played chess with Lord Underwood and argued over which course of action to take when he was fit for travel—the latter advocating armed insurrection, he a peaceful discussion with the King—and ate liquid foods and read the Northern poets.

On his sixth day, the hosting king, accompanied by two giant servants, came to express his happiness at the pace of Lord Dempsey's recovery, and to extend an invitation for him to stay as long as he liked and perhaps enjoy a hunting expedition in the foothills of Mount Matteson.

"Thank you, I will not forget this kindness, but we must return tomorrow."

The elderly monarch stared at the layered bandages covering Lord Dempsey's body. "We hope you will do us the honor of taking home a collection of our soft cheeses."

"That is most generous of you."

The two smiled at each other while a slick black dachshund scratched at the door and moaned for egress. "We are not unaware of the influence you wield at home, especially with your king."

"It has been some time since my king and I were together regularly."

"Nevertheless, you and he have a history of friendship."

"That is true."

The Northern king swayed in place and was instantly supported by his servants, who lowered him onto a chair. "There is something we would like to discuss with you, then, if we may."

"Certainly."

"Although it is not generally known, we have scrofula and must soon abdicate our throne. Because we haven't a son, the next in line for succession is our nephew, Amberson, who despite his reputation as an idler and popinjay is in fact an angry, violence-prone young man." The Northern king placed a hand over his eyes and looked as peaked as the convalescent. "I mention this because your king is preparing to attack us, and if he does Amberson has promised to respond by waging total warfare. No matter how modest or justified your invasion, he will lead our army on full-scale raids to lay waste your villages, farms, and city, to rape and plunder and turn what might have been a brief skirmish into protracted destruction. It is not hard to imagine the near-complete annihilation of our neighboring kingdoms within a few years. To avoid such an outcome, I ask you to urge your sovereign to abandon his war plans."

Lord Dempsey, sweating in the room's heat, his hair thickly pasted to his forehead, trembled in unison with his pale visitor. "I will relay your message, but there can be little hope of success so long as you allow rivers that have from time immemorial flowed through our land to be channeled to the West. If war results and your nephew escalates the conflict, the onus will fall squarely on you."

"We offered your king a chance to pay more than the West for river privileges, and he refused."

"You demanded two hundred thousand ducats a year for what had formerly been both free and in accord with nature's design."

The Northern king's voice hoarsened. "We have the same right to profit from our water as you do from your forests, which are more abundant than ours. And why should the West, which hitherto lacked any regular waters, suffer for what is as much nature's caprice as her design?"

"Our forests are more plentiful than yours because we did not cut them down in a paroxysm of greed forty years ago. Besides, the West has a fifth of our population and profligately wastes the water for lack of which our people are now starving and rioting."

The Northern king stood up. "I will not trouble or argue with you further. If you care about your people, you will do what is right."

"We are as one in that belief."

The next day, on the muddy road south, Lord Underwood, gazing out the carriage window, said that the King had not responded to Lord Dempsey's message about going north for medical treatment, which was further proof that there could be no rapprochement between them, that Lord Dempsey had to lead a campaign against the crown, and that his victory in the court of popular opinion would render meaningless his loss in the court of a corrupt king. Lord Dempsey replied that peace and unity in the kingdom were vital at that moment and that he was sure the people wanted as much.

After entering the city through a broad gate of black steel, they were stalled at a road block of standing horses, parked carriages, pedestrians, and tethered livestock. Lord Underwood called through the window for an explanation from the driver, who answered that a mime performance was taking place up ahead. A man bearing a strong resemblance to Lord Dempsey, dressed in a ministerial orange and blue robe and wearing a feather cap, seated in the middle of a row of fellow mock lords on a cardboard wall, was applauding an imaginary game. The man rose for an ovation and then, after a dark figure wearing the King's purple ran past him, he teetered and fell face forward to the ground, and then, after a full minute of pounding drums, someone began to sing: *Humphrey Dempsey sat on a wall, Humphrey Dempsey had a great fall. All the King's horses and all the King's men couldn't put Humphrey together again.* When the chorus started up again, more voices joined in, until soon everyone in the street was singing it and growing louder and more enthusiastic with each pass. Men slung their arms around each other and women pigeoned their heads back and forth and children clasped hands and spun around in circles screaming: *HUMPHREY DEMPSEY SAT ON A WALL! HUMPHREY DEMPSEY HAD A GREAT FALL!*

Lord Underwood held his breath and stared out the window. "It's a miracle. There's no use debating now; the revolution is about to begin, and we didn't even have to launch the first salvo! As though God Himself has decreed it—a stampede of popular support—driver!" He banged on the roof and shouted for the carriage to press forward—they must make Lord Dempsey's presence known so that he could give a speech—and then turned to his friend, whose seat was empty.

Over the next twenty-four hours, the King gave two public addresses. In the first he lamented the disappearance of Lord Dempsey, who apparently had run away because he was, and it grieved the King to say this, for he had loved him like a brother and was saddened by this revelation, an egg. No one knew how he had perpetrated this deceit for so long, but the fact was indisputable—for this reason and no other the King's doctors had been unable to heal him—and it thus stood to reason that his work in the House of Lords, the so-called Dempsey reforms, although on the surface judicious and laudable, had been proposed and pushed through the House of Lords for dubious, perhaps unnatural, ends. The King's second address stated that the Grain Dispensation Act, the Gendarme Deed, and the Landowner Retribution were temporarily suspended pending further review, and that the Aqueduct Plan's vote would be postponed. Which did *not* mean a return to intolerable living conditions for the people. The King's advisors had written up an official declaration of war against the North that he would sign the next day, and afterward he would personally lead the army to victory over their thieving neighbor, thereby restoring the two rivers to their rightful banks and ending the water shortage that afflicted the kingdom.

After the first speech, someone in the audience cried out that Lord Dempsey was no more an egg than his mother, the venerable Lady Dempsey, was a chicken, and they would not abide his being maligned in this ill-spirited, absurd fashion. If the King did not immediately produce Lord Dempsey, the greatest friend and champion of the people who'd ever lived, they would storm the castle and behead everyone inside. Three of the King's armed guard later sustained serious injuries keeping out the mob, among whom eighty-seven were wounded, and the King himself went into tremors and had to be laid out naked on his bed with a fan boy and water bearer at his side. After the second speech, delivered to an audience stuffed with royal plants who applauded the King's every fifth word, a cheer was started up to crush the North and bring back the rivers. The non-planted audience members, however, incensed at both the call for war and the King's continued failure to produce Lord Dempsey, attacked the royal sympathizers, and in the resulting melee another two hundred and seven people were injured.

In the middle of the night, the King heard a noise and opened his eyes on the pitch of his bedchamber. Judging by the position of the moon, it was after two in the morning. He lit and touched a match to a candle, whereupon a tall figure in the shadows sprang into view beside the open window.

"You!" said the King, sitting up in bed and drawing the covers high over his chest.

Lord Dempsey stepped forward and said, "I'm here to relay a message to you from the Northern king."

When he finished speaking, the King thanked him for the communication and said, "We'd like to apologize for not going to you after your fall, but Stanton and Caldwell promised us that it was a minor injury and that you would be back in the House of Lords within a week. As soon as we discovered its gravity and that Terryton was responsible, we put him to death, not to disguise our tracks but to punish a horrible act of which we had neither foreknowledge nor approval."

Lord Dempsey nodded.

"And we are sorry for calling you an egg. One of our physicians, who swung with Terryton the next day, had the temerity to claim as much, and although the nonsense should never have been repeated, our advisers convinced us that you are actively opposed to the state and should be discredited with the people. They repeated that you intended to start a revolution so many times that we felt we hadn't a choice." The King looked at his visitor plaintively and said, "You don't know what it's like to be surrounded by people who cast aspersions on those you love. One begins to lose perspective. But please know that our personal feelings for you have not changed."

"I don't care what you call me or accuse me of, and I would be prepared to publicly attest my loyalty to you now as always, but when we were children you said you'd never let your people go hungry, and you promised not to continue the policy of war your father followed during his reign. It's the wholesale betrayal of those pledges that upsets me."

The King's voice rose. "Did we legislate a drought or ask the North to divert our rivers? Is it our fault that we can't afford to dispense more than five hundred pounds of bread a day, or that the police, to maintain order, have had to use forceful measures against our subjects? And as long as we're discussing childhood vows, what about yours to uphold and protect our court? You talk about public avowals of loyalty, but ever since entering the House of Lords you've made us appear to be an avaricious, stupid despot."

"I am less responsible for that portrait than you."

The two were breathing heavily, separated by fifteen feet of cold marble floor, with a single flickering flame to illuminate and cast them in shadows, as wind from outside filled the window curtains like ship sails. Lord Dempsey's gloved hands were in fists, and the King's bedcovers had fallen to reveal his flushed neck and face. A minute passed and they relaxed by degrees, staring at each other with a combination of anger and love.

"To think how close we once were," said the King, "and how aligned were our thoughts!" He brushed at the folds of his bedsheet but failed to smooth them away. "So they might have continued, if not for politics."

Lord Dempsey smiled sadly. "It is more than politics when innocent people's lives are at stake." Turning around, he walked to the windowsill and rested a foot on the purple davenport beneath it. "Will you agree not to declare war on the North tomorrow, but instead to negotiate for the return of the rivers? Two hundred thousand ducats a year might wound your pride, but it would save your people immeasurable suffering."

The King, looking up, his body half-moving to stand and bridge the distance between them before falling back, nodded.

"Then all is not lost."

At that moment, Lords Underwood, Eltherington, and Paley were sending town criers and provocateurs to spread the rumor that Lord Dempsey had been abducted and killed by the King. Full-throated men went from village to farm to outlying pub, inciting their listeners to reject the call for war with the North and instead to unite their energies against the King, as bloodthirsty a tyrant as had ever sat on the throne. For who had, through his parsimony and negligence, allowed the rivers to be diverted? The King! And who had offered insufficient bread to feed thousands of hungry families? The King! And who had fought Lord Dempsey's generous, valiant reforms, each of which lightened the people's burden and put food in their pantries and sought to maximize what few resources the land had left? The King!

By dawn hundreds of thousands of people thronged the streets of the city, trying to get close to the public square, where Lord Underwood was to make their case for revolution and officially demand the King's head on a stake. Choruses of "Humphrey Dempsey sat on a wall, Humphrey Dempsey had a great fall" rose and fell spontaneously, mixed in with "Down with the King!" and "Send tyranny to the devil!" At eight o'clock, Lord Underwood, in the company of

Lords Eltherington, Sainsbury, Farrington, and Wessex, flanked by a legion of the standing army that had decided in a midnight parlay to transfer their allegiance to the House of Lords, strode onto a balcony overlooking the crowd and spoke on the evils of their current monarch, recapitulating the criers' arguments and adding new ones. Full of references to the Lord Dempsey he knew personally, a wise and great-souled man—a saint!—who, if he were there, would powerfully refute the King's pathetic attempt to brand him an egg and excuse a criminal war, his speech ended with a peroration on the people's responsibility to both themselves and to their fallen advocate, Lord Dempsey, to depose the King.

"Who's with me?" shouted Lord Underwood.

"We are!" bellowed the crowd.

"I can't hear you for the blood in my ears. Who's with me?"

"We are!"

"Who?"

"We are!"

Jostling in the square led to enthusiastic shoves and fists stabbing the air, followed by a deafening rendition of "Humphrey Dempsey sat on a wall, Humphrey Dempsey had a great fall. All the King's horses and all the King's men couldn't put Humphrey together again," at the end of which Lord Underwood raised a glinting sword above his head and pointed it toward the castle and was about to scream for them to charge when, from an opposing balcony across the square, a figure in a ministerial orange and blue robe appeared.

Confusion quickly segued into reverent awe, as the awareness spread that it was Lord Humphrey Dempsey, alive. The silence was nearly as sweeping as the noise had just been.

"Good people," said Lord Dempsey, when he had their attention. "In times of chaos, it can be difficult to pick out the notes of caution that are perforce quieter than those of action, but I beg you to listen. Now is no time to discount what little reason is still available to us, for we are poised, for the first time in our history, to destroy ourselves through either revolution or war. The question, which is as awful for a nation as for an individual to ask, seems to be: How do we want to die? At the hands of our brothers or at those of our neighbors to the north? Given the general momentum of this morning, and how my name has been used by my friends in the House of Lords to incite you against the King, this apparently is a Hobson's Choice. I do not blame you for leaning toward the most expedient form of suicide. I understand the impulse, born of hunger and frustration and the institutional rot of governing bodies, to charge headlong into the abyss, out of which will come, before the first shoots of grass grow from the present King's grave, merely another vessel of power that will in due course grow as many horns and fangs as it can be argued all rulers display. I believe, however, that we as a people have the option of a third way, one which lacks the flash and filigree of battle but has a compensatory beauty. One which allows for a future dry of the blood and tears that will otherwise drown us all long before the restoration of any rivers can water our crops. I propose, my friends and countrymen, a way of peace. I propose that you lower your swords and spears, that you put away your quivers and sharp stones, and that you go home to your families and continue the arduous task of survival, which is, I am here to tell you, about to become easier. I spoke with the King last night, and he has promised to pay the North what they are asking for water rights to the two rivers. This will in no way be an admission that the North had the moral or legal right to take them away from us in the first place, and it does not preclude the King from using his influence to someday reduce or eliminate the annual fee, but for now it will spare us the terror and torment of war, and it will return to you your livelihoods, and it will allow us to focus our thoughts and energies on improving the lives of everyone in the kingdom."

When Lord Dempsey stopped to breathe—he appeared fatigued and disoriented, shuffling awkwardly two steps to the left on his balcony—a man in the known employ of the King's advisers shouted, from the edge of the crowd, "He lies! He's nothing but an egg!" followed by a volley of refutations and demands that the King and his henchmen be put to death. Lord Dempsey gripped the railing in front of him and called out for quiet, for order, for reason to be given its due before emotions swept them all into a nightmare from which they would not emerge, and then, unnoticed at first by anyone but the two most directly involved, a rock sailed through the air and hit Lord Dempsey in the arm. Then another rock flew after the first and hit its mark, and another and another, by which time everyone had stopped and turned up to watch their hero reduced to a thousand irregular white shards floating down upon them like confetti, revealing absolutely nothing on the inside.

What came next hardly warrants retelling, so familiar is the story of how the King, when he learned of Lord Dempsey's fate, locked himself in his bedchamber and didn't emerge until the Northern army, which eventually routed his own armed forces, marauded through the land under the command of Amberson and left scorched ground and embers and salted earth in its wake, and finally arrived at the King's stronghold—where Caldwell and Stanton, whose efforts to cast Lord Dempsey as an abomination against nature had successfully redirected the people's anger from the Crown to his allies in the House of Lords, had brought to a permanent end the Dempsey reforms and trained the nation's wrath on the North—and stormed the castle and killed everyone but the King, whom they carried north in a triumphal march through his decimated land, past his emaciated, half-dead former subjects, and then through those parts of the North that had, when the war was not yet decided, themselves been scourged. Nor need the King's final posture be recounted, his kneeling before the Northern king as a sentence of death was read aloud to the ecstatic mass of Northern people assembled at his back, as he whispered to himself, "There is no north. There is no north. There is no north."

BANG

Kylie was named after an Australian pop singer who'd starred in *Neighbours*, a show about the furtive sex lives of twelve tri-toned Melburnians. Kylie's mother had gone to Australia after college and eaten spiced lamb curry, witchetty grubs, and a super-meringue called pavlova. She also scored ketamine in a Sydney park and slept with a tour guide and bought a letterpress journal in which she told her future child that pretty places were like pretty people, best admired from afar.

Twenty-four years later, Kylie lived in an apartment complex with two roommates, Armando and Rick, who went out one day and didn't come back. Someone who wrote online image captions, G.K. Chesterton, said that the man who killed a man killed a man, but the man who killed himself killed all men as far as he was concerned. Kylie drank Armando's oolong tea and thought of Armando wet from a shower, wet from kickboxing, wet from night terrors. She stared out her window at a smoky sunset and didn't touch herself with feeling.

The cryogenicists were already frozen in vaults and the Survivors had banded together in convention centers, city halls, and sports arenas, keeping watch over each other. The President and Vice-President were gone, as were the Speaker of the House and Senate Majority Leader and

Attorney General, leaving in charge the Majority Whip, who blamed the Disorder on a water-borne pathogen that stormed the blood-brain barrier, and whose first act as leader of the dwindling Free World had been to forbid drinking tap water, which made no difference.

The Disorder began in early June, when so many people jumped off a high-rise rooftop in Denver that witnesses described seeing a human waterfall. After similar incidents in San Antonio and Paris and Beijing, authorities sealed off access to rooftops across the planet but couldn't keep people from guns, aspirin, nooses, car crashes, slit wrists, blows to the head, strychnine, starvation, stabbings, drownings in bathtubs and lakes and rivers and reservoirs and oceans and swimming pools, carbon monoxide poisoning, unplugged life support machines, discarded insulin, snapped necks, etc.

Before Kylie moved in with Armando and Rick, her mother said, "Rick would be good to you, but not Armando. Attractive men are predators. I know you don't want to hear this, but I'm trying to protect you." Kylie listened dutifully and impatiently, because living with two guys didn't mean she had to fuck one or both of them. Her mother came from a generation that saw sex everywhere and in everything, as mystics saw God—a generation that despite its progressive bent was as blinkered and prurient as the Victorians, and Kylie wondered at what point people went from rejecting their elders' advice to dispensing it.

There were many theories about the Disorder. Some thought it flipped a switch in the brain that turned one's desire to live into its opposite. Others thought it caused excruciating mental and physical anguish or shut down the amygdala or stripped away one's illusions so that one could no more live happily than one could stare at the sun without going blind.

Alone in her apartment, Kylie thought about the brass bands she couldn't hear in the distance. Where had they gone, exactly? If,

as noted epidemiologist Joseph Stalin said, one death was a tragedy and a million deaths was a statistic, then nine billion deaths
was incomprehensible. She finished her tea and pictured Armando
shining his shoes, eating eggs, ignoring a talking head in the corner. Before going out with Rick one day, he had been training for
a national kickboxing competition, the Queen's Cup Celebration
in Anaheim, California, where he'd expected to weigh in at 160
pounds and fight in the controversial "no headgear" bracket. Rick
had often warned him about concussions while Kylie read a history
of Tasmania—the boat building, the massacres, the mashed food
diet—to no avail.

When Kylie realized that Armando and Rick weren't coming back
because they'd either joined the Survivors or run away or ended their
lives, she went into Armando's room and found a collection of pressed
flowers, a record of kickboxing fights in North America dating back to
2018, monogrammed cufflinks in sterling silver, and a wood carving
of Don Quixote that might have been a paperweight. He'd been married before, and he liked word puzzles and pictures of a dog named
Hafez. Kylie left the room thinking of a boy she once loved whose
father owned a shipping company in the Northeast and whose mother,
after divorcing his father, took up with another owner of a Northeast
shipping company. When the boy turned eighteen and got interested
in moonbeam technology, Kylie stopped loving him.

The avant-garde composer David Livingstone had said, "I am
prepared to go anywhere, provided it be forward," as had Kylie, although she no longer knew what going forward meant. The oolong
tea turned bitter and the outside stench of bodily decay and food
decay made opening the window impossible. Fires burned across the
city from electrical shortages and untended stovetops and oil refinery
explosions, and a thousand car alarms wailed out of sync. Wolf packs
roamed the streets eating stray dogs.

As a child, Kylie had sometimes hidden in her bedroom closet and pretended to be the last person on Earth, pretended that the kids who ignored her at school, the gear-grinding teachers, the effeminate mothers, the effeminate fathers, the firemen, the sloe-eyed crossing guards—that all of them were dead. The scope of her solitude had been dizzying. Anticipation possessed her like a fever. She hadn't dared move and risk dislodging the feeling. Hours of her eight- and nine-year-old life had passed in vibrating silence.

One night, as an adult in her shared apartment, Kylie had sat at the kitchen island cutting her pills in two when Rick left to talk to his sponsor and Armando stepped out of the bathroom, fresh from a shower. He stood next to her and frowned and flexed the muscles of his right forearm. "I get them in a stronger dosage than I need to save money," she explained, guillotining a pill in her tiny blade contraption and sliding the half-moon pill pieces into a chalky pile. She scraped the half moons into a translucent orange bottle and twisted its cap on and stood up and sidestepped Armando, whose grip on the towel around his waist loosened, and went into her room and locked the door and put a hand over her racing heart and turned on music low enough so that Armando, if he were outside with his ear pressed against the door, would hear but not recognize the loose guitar stylings of Sonny Sharrock, and she wasn't a prisoner in her own home even though an impartial observer might see her that way, as a prisoner, and she wished she had something to eat, a piece of bread or jar of peanut butter, and she looked around for her phone and heard the floorboards outside her room creak and imagined her door bursting open and sat on the edge of her bed, angry that an observer might see her as a prisoner and angry that they might be right.

It was now a week since Kylie last talked to her mother, who'd said, "The line of cars headed to the Grand Canyon is a hundred miles long, like when we evacuated to Houston for Hurricane Vishnu. Do you remember that, the gridlock? But you were only six. I feel normal except I don't have an appetite. I know I should eat but putting something in my mouth seems pointless, like feeding a doll. Why don't you go to the convention center? I'd feel better knowing you were with the Survivors, even if it's true about the rapes and assaults." Kylie hung up and was packing a bag when Rick, standing in her doorway, said that if the Disorder was caused by a contagion, the Lifer encampments would all be infected soon. Kylie's and Rick's and Armando's best bet was to stay where they were.

From the beginning, Kylie had known that neither bacteria nor viruses had caused the Disorder. And that no switch in the brain could be flipped to make someone want to die. Imagine. She stared out at the plumes of smoke and the deserted streets and the charred buildings and the overgrown lawns and the absence—the displacement—of love. Should she read a book? Open a can of soup? Were wildflowers blooming all over the country, and did rivers—did the Mississippi itself—run free of pesticides and nitrogen for the first time in a hundred years? She could walk to Lake Pontchartrain, *que sera, sera.*

Four days earlier, she'd said to her roommates, "There's only enough food for a couple more days. Let's go to a supermarket." Rick said he and Armando would do it together. That way, if it was a contagion, only the two of them would die, and Kylie would have triple the food rations. She argued without conviction that that was a sexist plan, and when they left she bolt-locked the door and watched the clock until they'd been gone long enough to have returned.

Alone in her apartment now, she took off her clothes in front of a mirror. She couldn't find anything wrong with her body and pulled out the tie from her ponytail and her hair cascaded over her shoulders and grazed her breasts. Everyone knew about the beauty of Helen because Bauhaus denier Homer had written, "Was this the face that launched a thousand ships / And burnt the topless towers of Ilium?" which forever changed the nature of love and shipbuilding and *casus belli*. Kylie sang one of her namesake's biggest hits, "I Should Be So Lucky," and did a kind of pompom shake around her living room, *so lucky lucky lucky*, and wondered if a country founded by criminal exiles on the backs of sun-baked aborigines could have evolved into paradise if given more time. She returned to the window and the dark city was a wash of pink red black.

Not being a prisoner on the night Armando stood beside her in the kitchen in a towel, Kylie had opened her bedroom door and gone to his room, where he lay on his bed staring at the ceiling. "Can't sleep?" she asked. "I'm going to lose my fight in Anaheim," he said. She opened her bottle of pills and shook two half-moons into his palm. "What're these?" he asked. "They get rid of bad thoughts," she said. He put them in his mouth and chewed, not grimacing, and said, "They can tell bad thoughts from good?"

A month after the Disorder began and a week after she last spoke to her mother and four days after her roommates left, Kylie walked out the front door and ascended the stairwell to the unbarricaded rooftop of her building. Looped around the perimeter railing was a pair of handcuffs with a body attached. She looked at a row of bejeweled rings, a bloodless arm, an intricate paisley pattern of shirtsleeve, and then closed her eyes.

"It is sometimes just at the moment when we think everything lost that the intimation arrives which may save us," said bobbysoxer Marcel Proust, though Kylie intimated nothing and expected not to be saved. She went to the edge of the rooftop and peered down at the abandoned cars on the street below. One minute everyone was going about their furtive sexual business and the next they were lining up to die. Kylie, naked, felt the swamp air like invisible dust and swung her legs over the railing and thought of Armando swallowing the pills and asking her to lie down on the bed next to him, and her backing away in horror not at the invitation, but at how her mother would have wanted her to back away. Kylie selected one of the cars, a shadowy rectangle, and, thinking of the great dramaturge Haile Selassie's question, "We have finished the job, what shall we do with the tools?" aimed an untentative

SUNRISE

The Woman from the city boards a train that takes her to a boat that conveys her to a village. She rents a room at the inn for a week but stays two months. The villagers wonder from what or whom she's hiding.

One night she lights a cigarette from the candle burning in her room and brushes her short auburn hair one-two-three, one-two-three, then slips a thin dress over her thin frame, powders her ashen face, and in the common room tells the Innkeeper's Wife to shine her black shoes. The Innkeeper's Wife puts down her needlework to oblige the Woman, who smokes with her chin held high, as if posing for a portrait.

On the other side of the village, the Husband sits expressionless at home until he hears the Woman whistle outside. He flashes a half-mad smile and his Wife enters the room with two place settings, her straight golden hair drawn into a complicated braid. She arranges the settings in front of and opposite him, then leaves the room and returns a moment later with a serving bowl to find him gone.

Two Old Women in a nearby courtyard fold wind-stiffened clothes—it's late for this task—and discuss the Husband and Wife: "They used to be like children, laughing and playing." The Old Women sigh for the Husband and Wife, and for every other couple that no longer laughs and plays like children.

Along a wide path bordered by tall bulrushes, the Husband walks to the lake with his arm around the Woman who is not his Wife. Through a break in the clouds they can see the bright, cratered moon and a starless patch of sky.

At home, the Wife sinks onto the bench where her Husband sat. She does not hear Baby crying in a corner of the room or Grandmother saying that a storm is on its way.

The Husband and Woman embrace on the shore of the lake.

"Tell me you're mine," she says.

"I'm yours," he says.

"Then come with me to the city."

He looks down. "What about my Wife?"

Pressing him to her chest and cradling his lowered head, the Woman murmurs, "She might drown."

The Husband pulls away and shakes her violently and throws her to the ground. She gets up and describes the city in vivid, quadraphonic detail, in three dimensions augmented by sound. He can hear a jazz combo and see a bandleader in a pinstriped suit jumping up and down while on a ballroom floor men and women are kinetic motion, their bodies swaying back and forth, their legs swinging in synchrony. The Woman dances in front of the Husband and he begins to feel it, to understand, and he pulls her back to the ground, this time in excitement rather than anger.

When it's over, she gathers bulrushes and tells him to use them to stay afloat after he overturns the boat carrying his Wife. Then she stashes them, bound, in the boat's hull.

The Husband later tiptoes into his bedroom, where his Wife lies on a narrow bed. He stretches out on the adjacent narrow bed without undressing.

His Wife does not move. Is she asleep? Has all this been a bad dream, and she'll awake in the morning relieved that a future in which she and her Husband never again laugh or play like children, in which secrets are held more tightly than beliefs, can be avoided?

The next day, unshaven, hair aslant, in rumpled clothes, the Husband suggests to his Wife that they go away for the day, just the two of them. She is slow to realize that he wants to be alone with her for what can only be one reason, but when she does, overjoyed, she spins Baby round and round, and tells Grandmother that she and her Husband won't be home until late.

His head bowed and his shoulders hunched forward, the Husband walks behind his Wife to the lake where the night before he lay with the Woman under a cratered moon and starless sky. Along the way they pass a dog that barks and strains against the chain tethering it to a stake in the ground. At the dock, the Wife settles into the boat and her Husband attaches the oars, unties the mooring, and launches them onto the water.

Meanwhile the dog uproots its stake in the ground, races to the shore, and swims out to the boat. The Wife lifts it up and accepts its frantic attention, its licking and panting and pawing. The Husband grimly reverses course and drags the barking dog back onto the land, where he drives its tethering stake deep into the ground.

His Wife has never seen the dog so upset. Should she get off the boat? She stands and looks around. Everything is fine. She sits back down and smooths her dress and there is a heavy stillness on the water and in the air. She examines the tumescent sky. *Is* everything fine?

Before she can answer, her Husband returns and resumes rowing. When they reach the middle of the lake, too far away to be seen by anyone on land, he lets go of the oars and the boat drifts in a half-circle.

His Wife says solicitously, nervously, "You must be tired."

For a moment he is as still as the water and air. Then he slowly rises to his feet and without speaking moves toward her with outstretched, claw-like hands. The boat yaws gently side to side. There is no atmospheric disturbance. She cowers in her seat and shuts her eyes as he reaches down to cause the accident that will end her life.

Instead, he drops his hands to his sides and backs away and drops to his seat. Neither understands what's happened. Is it his conscience? A failure of nerve? Or has he been released from the spell of the Woman from the city, under which he fell as easily, as heedlessly as anyone who wants more than he needs and no more of what he has?

When they arrive on the other side of the lake, his Wife, from her coiled, huddled position, springs out of the boat and disappears into the woods.

Her Husband follows, shouting, "Don't fear me!"

At the rail tracks running along the edge of the woods, she hops onto a trolley car and sits on a wooden bench surrounded by passengers reading and talking and staring through the windows at pine trees spaced as uniformly as street lamps. She will make sense of this later. She is safe from her Husband. She can relax.

But now her Husband leaps onto the back platform and squeezes through the passengers to take the seat next to her. "Don't fear me," he says again.

She turns away and sobs, in pain and confusion and terror. The other passengers say nothing. How many times have they too been hurt in public, their desire to appear as they would like to be—in control, in situ—no match for the cruel words and cruel behavior of the one they love? And how many times have they been the loved one who speaks and behaves cruelly? Better to let this drama unfold as it must.

The trolley rattles on and the Wife grows calmer, grows numb. Once in the city she steps down onto a street overrun with automobiles, bicycles, pedestrians. She walks blindly through the loud, frenetic traffic and enters a restaurant and sits at a corner table and doesn't acknowledge her Husband when he comes to plead for a third time, "Don't fear me!"

A Waiter delivers a plate of bread. The Husband places a slice in his Wife's hand and she lifts it mechanically to her mouth, then drops it to the floor as a final sob passes through her, as meaningless as a yawn. When he reaches down to pick it up, she leaves the restaurant and stands on the sidewalk, where cars and buses and trolleys speed by, flashes of heavy machinery.

Her Husband appears and says the thing he can't stop saying, "Don't fear me," but this time instead of a command or a plea, it sounds like an invocation.

She could step in front of a speeding bus as easily and heedlessly as she could push him in front of one.

Across the street a Bride and Groom ascend the red-carpeted steps of a church through a swarm of wedding guests. It looks like a coronation. The Husband buys a bouquet of flowers from a Street Vender and gives it to his Wife. Holding the bouquet carelessly, she walks over to the wedding. Inside the church, she sits on a back pew. Her Husband finds a spot beside her as the Groom repeats his vows, "…I will protect her from all harm…." The Husband grips his Wife's wrist and the words echo in his head, "…I will protect her from all harm…I will protect her from harm…." and he cries and releases his Wife's wrist. He understands, at last, that he has forfeited his right to touch her, that she must abhor him, that his desires, embodied by the Woman from the city but emanating from a damaged part of himself that differs in degree but not kind from that of other people, are hereafter irrelevant. He feels this like a burning sensation with no point of origin. The Bride and Groom exchange rings at the altar, and the wedding guests lean in closer as if love were an aroma, and the Husband wipes away his tears with the sleeve of his coat. He trembles as if feverish. When his Wife looks at him she sees a man she thought she knew but doesn't, not completely. Maybe complete knowing is impossible. And maybe the danger she faced earlier was just a variation of the danger intrinsic to love. Death comes in many forms. She draws her Husband to her chest and cradles his head, murmuring, "There, there." His tears fall rapidly and he says, "Forgive me!" and links his arms around her waist. She watches the wedding ceremony now as if it were not a coronation, but a rehearsal bearing little resemblance to its future performances. The organ music moves up a scale, the minister extols the Bride and Groom, and in between every sunrise and sunset is a light that cannot be extinguished.

The Wife and Husband leave the church and wander blindly down the sidewalk until they come to a barber shop where she points out his reflection in the window. They laugh at his scruffiness and go inside, where a cavalier Barber slathers shaving cream on the Husband's face while the Wife sits in the waiting area with a magazine. Beside her a Man holds a newspaper. The Barber scrapes off the Husband's beard with a bone-handled razor, each flick of his wrist as graceful as a conductor's, and points to a picture taped to the mirror: a famous actor. With a sidelong glance, the Man in the waiting room adjusts his newspaper and lays an elbow on the Wife's arm. She frowns and moves away from him, eager for her Husband to return. The Man leans over to whisper in her ear.

The Husband returns to the waiting area and preens in front of his Wife. She stands and caresses his smooth face and says *How handsome*. The Man with the newspaper accuses her of leading him on and says the Husband should keep her on a leash. She raises her hand to slap the Man, who shrinks back—who cowers—as the Husband looks on with surprise and admiration. His Wife spits on the Man and leads her Husband out through the revolving doors.

Night is falling as they come to the county fair, which has a Ferris Wheel, rollercoasters, magicians, mermaids, fortune tellers, and games of skill. People stream through the gate in both directions, eating tufts of cotton candy with prizes tucked under their arms. At the Pig in a Poke booth, the Husband hands money to the Game Operator and is given five balls. He pitches them at a small ring ten feet away and lands one on his fifth throw, whereupon a tiny pig slides down a shoot to land at the Operator's feet.

The Operator shakes the Husband's hand, tells him to select a stuffed animal, and bends down to put the pig back on its overhead platform, but the pig is slippery and squirms free and darts through the legs of a delighted crowd.

The Husband and Wife chase the pig across the fairgrounds, dodging children and starry-eyed teenagers, to a banquet hall where they stop to catch their breath and lean against a crepe-papered wall.

Inside the adjacent kitchen, a Pastry Chef finishes a bottle of wine and opens a new one. The kitchen is clean and orderly, with pots and pans hanging from wall hooks in a line of descending size. He takes a swig and closes his rheumy eyes, the better to feel the wine's warmth.

A moment later he sees a tiny pig looking up at him. He shakes his head to clear away the vision, but the pig remains. The Chef drops the bottle and it shatters on the ground. The pig excitedly drinks the spilled wine, its hooves struggling for purchase on the slippery floor, and the Chef backs out through the kitchen doors, where the Husband and Wife, passing by, stop to look in.

Tiptoeing into the kitchen as lightly as he had into the bedroom the night before, the Husband seizes the tipsy pig and returns to the banquet hall holding it aloft like a trophy. Everyone cheers and presses in on the Husband and Wife. The Chef makes a jubilant, incoherent speech.

There are calls for the Husband and Wife to dance. They refuse until the Bandleader, a tall man in a pinstripe suit, lifts his baton and a jazz combo starts to play. The Wife and her Husband sway together slowly and then ecstatically as the tempo picks up, their legs swinging back and forth synchronously, their bodies kinetic motion.

When the music ends, the Chef makes another jubilant, incoherent speech, the pig squeals, the crowd applauds, and the Wife and Husband wave joyfully.

It is growing late, so the Husband and Wife bid farewell to the Bandleader, the Game Operator, the Chef, and take the next trolley back to the edge of the woods, where they walk to the lakeshore and kiss, at first chastely and then passionately.

In the boat, the Husband takes up the oars and gazes lovingly at his Wife, who lies back with her chin held high, as if posing for a portrait.

Rain begins when they reach the middle of the lake, a few drops that turn into a steady downpour that turns into a torrent. Winds agitate the surface of the lake and lightning strikes nearby and there is rolling thunder. The Husband's rowing grows difficult. Waves crest and fall, tossing the boat about heedlessly.

The Husband, his eyes stinging from the rain and his arms aching, grabs the bundle of bulrushes stored in the boat's hull and tells his Wife to hold onto it in case she is thrown overboard. She shouts above the howling wind that she won't do so unless he has one, too, but before he can answer a wave knocks the boat over and tosses them into the roiling, turbulent water.

At sunrise, the Husband, lying prone in wet clothes on wet sand, regains consciousness. He staggers to his feet and lopes up and down the shore calling for his Wife. Pieces of the shattered boat are strewn among the rocks.

He spies the bundle of bulrushes, then runs yelling along the path back to the village, where people come out of their houses—the Innkeeper's Wife, the Old Women, the Grandmother, the Woman from the city, villagers of all ages—and follow him to the lake. A lifeless body has washed ashore.

The Husband drops to his knees and buries his head in the body. The villagers do not comfort him. The Innkeeper's Wife steps forward and says that this is no accident, that she overheard her lodger, the Woman from the city, talking about it in her sleep.

The Husband, tears streaming down his face, says no, he and his Wife were in the boat together during last night's storm—he almost drowned himself—but the villagers know better. Hands seize the Woman from the city, who seems about to flee. Hands seize the Husband, who does not resist.

The march back to the village is silent. Sunlight plays on the marsh and the Husband's clothes dry unevenly. Already he needs another shave. Grandmother, who was once merely his Mother, cradles the Baby in her arms, crying softly, "What will happen to us now? Did they think of that, ever?"

AGAPE

After Pine Ridge split apart, I went back to Los Angeles to stay with my older brother, Saul, who'd once told me I could recover at his place when Pine Ridge failed (*Communes are like new restaurants, it's just a matter of time*), but his girlfriend was about to move in and she was sensitive to the biorhythms of other people (*We don't even eat together because the sound of my chewing bugs her. She's got misophonia and it's a real condition*), so I found a ground-floor sublet in an Art Deco midrise called Lyman Place. A one-room studio with an adjunct kitchenette and en suite bathroom, it had barred windows, beige carpeting, and travertine molding. It also had a wall-mounted ironing board that Andrea, the Hungarian life coach who'd lived there for three years, showed me when we met.

"This is a table to make your clothes flat," Andrea said, pulling open the cupboard door from which it folded down. Her mother was sick and she had to return to her hometown in Hungary, a village known for its suffused honey baklava, and she was having many visa troubles and didn't know how long she'd be away, at least a couple of months, and she would have to take her arthritic cat to the Humane Society because none of her friends were cat people.

I examined the board's torn and yellowed fabric, its daisy pattern flecked with red wine or blood stains.

"Not every place has this amenity," she said quietly, rubbing a small burn hole I hadn't noticed. "Newer apartments don't have it, certainly." While I raised and lowered the ironing board, she straightened her shoulders and said in a louder voice, "Also, the water is strong."

"Strong?"

"Let me show you."

She ran a hand through her thick hennaed hair, separating it into six plaits that didn't flow back into one, and motioned for me to walk through the door behind her. It was hard for us to stand in the bathroom without touching, so we leaned away from each other in a wishbone formation. Through an eye-level window I saw two hobos arguing in the alley beside a futon with bites taken out of its back cushion.

Andrea turned on the bath faucet and a shock-white stream of water beat down on the tub floor. We watched it for a moment before she said, "Now let me show you the garbage disposal," and cranked the faucet to its off position.

"No need," I said. "I'll take it."

Growing up, I'd wanted to get out of Los Angeles. On my way to school or Unitarian Universalist Church functions or the aerospace library or saxophone lessons, I'd look at the scrimmaged sky, endless asphalt and scorched stucco, at everything overexposed, and feel a dark, sinking sensation that never touched bottom. "It feels like a rundown mall, even the wealthy parts," I told an old summer camp friend from Chicago while visiting him in high school. "And it's hot all the time. I can't think clearly."

We were sitting on barstools at his kitchen counter, watching his mom sauté Chilean sea bass and listening to a sound collage. My friend said, "What's that a metaphor for?" His mom, who'd gone to art school at lilting Urbana-Champaign, added a splash of clear liquid that made the skillet sizzle and blackened the edges of the sea bass. "What's what a metaphor for?" I asked. "Heat," he said. "What's heat a metaphor for?" I said, "It was a hundred degrees in January." His mom's small, ovoid breasts rested below her sternum and she moved slowly, and I wondered under what set of conditions the impossible might become possible. My friend said that the whole world felt like a rundown mall and that heat was no barrier to clear thinking, that the ancient Greek philosophers had worked in a Mediterranean climate.

Maybe heat *was* a stand-in for deeper, more unsettling aspects of Los Angeles or myself than I could admit to, but it didn't matter because someday I'd move to a farm or small town or rural idyll up north and everything would be all right forever.

So when in college I heard that an Oregon commune called Pine Ridge had an opening for a new member, I submitted an application and underwent a trial living period during which the longest-term resident, Paul, and the most recent arrival, Dion, each took me aside to attack the other. In the herb garden under a gibbous moon Paul said that Dion was lazy and immature and trying to turn Pine Ridge into a stoner frat house, and in the kitchen with the radio blasting Dion said that Paul was uptight and inflexible and trying to turn Pine Ridge into boot camp. I nodded at both men and said I understood and shared their concerns. This didn't feel like lying or betrayal or suggestibility or schizophrenia or a craven effort to be accepted, and I began the life I'd dreamt about.

After I'd been at Lyman Place a few days, my brother called to say he'd gotten me an interview at his company, a media startup in Culver City. "It's entry-level," he said, "and the pay's hourly, but you could be doing what I do in a few years, which is a sweet fucking gig most of the time. In the interview just say you're excited about the power of cross-platform, vertically integrated media to change lives."

"I'm not excited about that."

"The interviewer's name is Mackenzie. We went out for a minute and it didn't work, but she's chill and the job's basically yours."

I set down my phone and opened the window above my bed. Snippets of outside conversations drifted in—*I want love on my own terms* and *Your knee ever pop when you're just sitting there?* and *People fussing about rotisserie chicken* and *We broke up because she learned to read minds*—and Pine Ridge had had virgin groves of Douglas firs and susurrant streams and wild grasses surrounding the greenhouse portico, which in early autumn glowed topaz at dawn and dusk, as well as cosplay days and sound bath nights and weekend classes on astronomy, horticulture, and sexual preparedness. It had helped shape my ideas about collaboration and responsibility, as if ideas were bonsais, so that I now understood why so many people didn't know what to do or how to do it or whether it was worth the mental and physical toll, *it* being *x* in the problem of modern life. Outside of Pine Ridge my bonsai ideas would soon become, without pruning and tethering, without Intention, a bramble.

But there was no going back to Pine Ridge, because Pine Ridge was dead and I had killed it.

When we were in elementary school, Saul invited me to be part of a club he'd started called the Cornerboys. Its mission was to spy on people. As the junior and only other member, I joined him in spying on our parents and neighbors and pedestrians and park-goers during what they thought were private moments. Mostly they did boring things, but sometimes they'd masturbate, crossdress, take drugs, self-injure, scream, make strange faces, pick at themselves, binge eat, vomit, cry, dance, and stare sightlessly into space. Because Saul was nine and I was six, we misinterpreted some of what we saw, but we grasped much of it—pleasuring and hurting oneself made sense—and as I got older my Cornerboy experiences led me to nod rather than recoil when people confessed their secrets. Nothing human was alien to me, and I listened and withheld judgment and earned others' trust and gratitude, though sometimes they got annoyed and angry and accusatory. Didn't I realize how fucked up it was when they dug razor blades into their arms? Snorted too much crank and puked up whole meals and choked themselves unconscious? Couldn't I distinguish a confession from a cry for help? I'd say that it wasn't my place to tell them what was right and wrong in their lives—they had to make those decisions themselves—and they'd say, *Yes, it is! When I delude myself or can't stop self-destructive behavior, I need you to set me straight! I need to be saved!*

But that was the problem: the belief that they or anyone could be saved. For life's difficulties were constant in degree if not in kind, and the fears and obstacles one faced as a child kept their intensity into adolescence even as they changed form and substance, just as they did into adulthood and old age and death, and the coping mechanisms one developed to deal with those fears and obstacles, however taboo, should, if successful, be accepted and even appreciated, the underlying truth being that all of this, and by all of this I meant Life, was so hard that temporary and possibly controversial fixes were the most we could hope for. That our time on Earth was no more—*though no less!*—than a stay of execution, so we should forgive ourselves our so-called degeneracy.

I didn't say that out loud, however, because the person I was talking to wouldn't have believed it. I myself didn't believe it. I saw the difference between healthy and unhealthy living. I condemned the boutiques of Beverly Hills and mansions of Malibu and Ferraris of the 405, the concentrated consumption and vanity surgeries and self-promotion and sunbathing and juice-cleansing that distracted people from—blinded them to—not only their everyday terrors, but the sense of community that was one of the few consolations we had. And I saw that, taken to its natural conclusion, my argument would have condoned anything—murder and rape and ecocide—as long as that thing made its practitioners feel better.

At Pine Ridge one day, I was picking weevils out of the grain bins in the pantry when Paul came in and said, "I've studied the history and inner workings of communes going back to Fourier, and the ones that make it are the ones that have well-defined rules and roles. I mean, listen, I don't hate a good time. There are nights when I want to play loud music after 10 p.m., too, but what if we all did that whenever we felt like it? There'd be music blaring every night of the week. I'd enjoy my nights but hate it the rest of the time. Respect is what it's about. Respecting other people's right to peace and quiet and cleanliness and the regular income Pine Ridge needs to get by."

On another day I was smoking weed with Dion on the riverbank when he said, "We don't need to spring clean the place every week or boost candle sales if it means working more. We should live with mess and live with less. Conservation and toleration. I'm not a lazy piece of shit, but I'm also not here for a nine-to-five workday. If someone needs a privatized, antiseptic life, they can get it on the outside. It's everywhere. Pine Ridge should be a refuge from that. Forget the chore chart and quiet hours schedule and trigger warnings before every conversation. We're adults. We're fucking adults. That's my point."

Both men said that my coming to Pine Ridge had been a godsend, that they no longer worried about the other one winning the war for Pine Ridge's soul because when things came to a head I would tip the numbers in their favor. With both I nodded and said, *Pine Ridge can be utopia.*

———

An actress named Jennifer lived across the hall from me at Lyman Place. She hadn't gotten any real parts because she had a crooked smile and symmetry was important to beauty and beauty was important to the entertainment industry.

"Or it could be something else," she said one morning when we dropped our garbage bags into the back alley dumpster. "Casting directors don't give you feedback unless they want to sleep with you, and then it's soft-pedaled."

We met again later in the mailroom, where we pulled from our mailboxes a glossy flyer appeal to help authorities locate Christina Scott James, a twelve-year-old abducted in Huntington Beach on her way home from a piano lesson, last seen riding a silver kick scooter and wearing gold-stitched bell bottom jeans, a "Wild Thing" T-shirt, and orthodontic headgear.

Jennifer looked at the girl's school portrait and said, "It's like in nature documentaries when a tiger attacks a gazelle and you think, *Holy shit, nature is evil and should be stopped.* This girl went from a piano lesson to a pervert's white van. It's horrible."

I agreed that it was horrible, but simple agreement wasn't enough in a situation like that, where two people in the safety of their own apartment complex talk about unknown violence done to someone purer and more vulnerable than themselves, so I added that the police would find Christina Scott James because this was a high-profile case—they'd already sent out three Amber alerts—and that the girl would be protected from permanent mental and emotional harm by the inner strength we had inherited from our earliest human ancestors, an inner strength developed by fleet groups of proto-people running from predators and chasing prey on the plains of northern Africa and steppes of central Asia.

"Wouldn't that be great?" Jennifer said, dropping the flyer into the recycling bin and heading out for a ride-hailing shift.

Pine Ridge had begun when Dev Upanishad, a timber baron whose company clear-cut large swaths of southwest Oregon's old-growth forests, wanted to make up for his life's work, like Alfred Nobel after inventing dynamite, by building a commune on a secluded piece of land near the Russian River and letting twelve strangers live there with him. Dev died in a whitewater rafting accident a year later, and over time the other original members drifted away because of love, boredom, illness, sharing fatigue, homesickness, hardening of their political arteries, religion, or job opportunities, and new residents took their places. Some of these newcomers respected the system in place and others didn't, and tensions arose over tradition and innovation, chaos and control, age and youth—over everything and nothing.

By the time I arrived, Paul and Dion embodied these tensions. Paul had short, tidy gray hair and wore brown cargo pants and denim shirts every day. Dion had a wavy, ringleted blond mane and large wardrobe of rainbow dashikis, linen culottes, and action sandals. Paul kept farming hours, ate steel-cut oatmeal and hardy grain bowls, stayed sober and celibate, and spoke in short, efficient sentences. Dion went to bed late and got up late, ate hot dogs and processed cereal, drank and did drugs, had indiscriminate sex, and told rambling, off-color stories. Half of Pine Ridge's residents lived like Paul, the other half like Dion.

I swung back and forth. Sometimes I'd run six miles at daybreak, work ten hours, and sleep alone, and sometimes I'd get high at noon, work a few hours, and sleep with a former bike messenger named Amelia who told me toward the end that our love was a baby version of love, soft and uninflected by time—that is, not hard, clear-eyed, and adult—which was okay as long as we didn't discuss the future hopefully or the past dismissively, to which I said that love, like God, couldn't be defined and that any attempt to capture it in words would leave us empty-handed, so that we needn't worry about what we could or couldn't say to each other, what might be allowed under the terms of love's agreement, for worrying would mean we knew what we were feeling, whereas no one ever really knew what they were feeling, hence the radical reversals and epiphanies that came at important moments of people's lives and made them think they'd figured themselves out at last, only to realize a little later that they'd been mistaken—*What was I thinking?*—which showed that their emotions were mysterious, shape-shifting phantasms best acted on with skepticism and caution and humility. Amelia slipped on an Elvis T-shirt and said, "I don't know what exactly's going on in your head, but if this place ever breaks apart you should go home and get help."

At the next week's house meeting, Paul announced that we'd sold too few candles that year to cover our property taxes, and that we needed to raise money quickly by borrowing from friends and family. Dion suggested we not pay our taxes because the government would use them to fund immoral wars and torture campaigns. Paul said we'd be fined and evicted if we didn't pay. Dion said we could hold off any federal agents who tried to make us leave. Paul said that would be reckless and possibly suicidal, and Dion accused him of being fearful and paranoid. They shouted at each other and others chimed in until Amelia called for silence and a folded-paper vote. There were six ayes, six nays, and one abstention. Everyone turned toward me.

The afternoon before my interview at Saul's company, I found Jennifer sitting on the front steps of Lyman Place, red-eyed because she hadn't gotten the part of Tabitha, a real estate agent by day and exotic dancer by night, in *The Tides of Love*.

"I read a monologue from the script they gave me," she said, "and I thought it was the best audition of my life." The straps of her sandals sparkled with encrusted jewels, and she wore a broad sun visor that hid her face. "Maybe you could watch it and tell me what I'm doing wrong? Do you have a minute?"

I sat on the sectional couch in her living room and ate dried fruit while she warmed up with long-vowel vocal exercises. Spoken by a very young woman to her very old protector, Jennifer's monologue began slowly, almost shyly—like a child telling her father that his temper scared her—and built into a loud, bitter, and transfixing assault on the pride of wealthy men for whom other people were either obstacles to overcome or playthings to discard.

"The show's called *The Waves of Love*?" I asked when she finished and broke character by rubbing her nose and massaging her throat.

"*The Tides of Love*. It's a new online soap opera."

"Is it good?"

"Kind of."

It was obvious why Jennifer hadn't gotten the part. Instead of just titillating her *Tides of Love* audience with the facile come-ons and flip cattiness of a regular soap opera character whose deceptions ruin lives and drain fortunes, she would have implicated her viewers in the high-stakes moral lottery that threatens to expose and bankrupt the whole soap opera world in any given scene on any given day. She would have made it personal by exposing the parallels between watcher and watched, the mutually dependent relationship between a Tabitha and a *Tides of Love* fan, which isn't to say that her character's existence would have depended on the show's viewership, which would have been decided by the regular attention of people who enjoyed Tabitha's pain and dissembling—rather it's to say that Jennifer's Tabitha and fan would have been in a symbiotic relationship requiring the real person's identification with the fictional character's need to appear stronger than she was in order to reap the benefits of power that would ultimately lead to disaster for herself and everyone else within three degrees of separation on the show, while provoking in the real person an unsettling mixture of satisfaction that justice had been served and horror that what made us feel most alive had such awful consequences.

"How should I have done it differently?" she asked. "Be honest."

I said she could've placed more emphasis on the words *digging*, *eighteen*, and *respect*, because I had to say something, and she bowed her head like she'd known it all along, and I returned to my apartment and listened to police helicopters keep a separate peace until dawn.

At my interview, Mackenzie, the Human Resources manager for Saul's company, apologized for not having looked at my CV because she'd spent the morning finding a replacement for an employee out with meningitis.

"Why don't you tell me your resume highlights?" she said. "Where you went to college, extracurriculars, internships, job history, that kind of thing."

As I talked, she leaned back in her wingback chair and massaged her wrists. Then she said, "Did you manage the commune's website or do community outreach? Anything relevant to social media content creation?"

"I mostly made candles."

"Huh." Her phone vibrated on her metal desk, a rumble-strip sound. "What do you like in terms of ad campaigns, TV shows, movies, short animation, virtual reality platforms, vines?"

"I don't watch much."

"Are you a gamer?"

"No."

"Who do you follow on social media?"

I shook my head.

"Favorite brands or CEOs or fashion designers or athletes?"

I shook my head.

She lowered the window blinds with her phone. "In many ways you're unqualified for this job, maybe in every way, and normally that'd be the end of the interview, but Saul went to bat for you so we can keep talking."

"Okay."

"The job's simple: you'd leak information about our clients' new releases, write positive consumer reviews of our clients' new releases using aliases, get our clients' new releases to trend, and coordinate fanboy responses."

"Responses to clients' new releases?"

"Mmm."

With twelve pairs of eyes on me at Pine Ridge, I had stood at the edge of a round room with a round table with beveled edges and said that the vote from which I'd abstained was about more than just whether to pay our property taxes. It was a referendum on two seemingly incompatible approaches to communal living that could in fact work together. Each had good qualities. Paul's order-and-organization approach provided group stability and se-curity—doing the same thing day after day established rhythms that, like heartbeats, were vital for survival—and Dion's relaxed approach gave us spontaneity and adaptability—improvising our days kept us from falling into the deadening rut of mindless rou-tine, which allowed us to grow as individuals. Reminding everyone that the definition of a first-rate mind was being able to hold two contradictory ideas and still function, I said we could create a new, holistic, inclusive, more perfect Pine Ridge by preserving while cor-recting for our differences. If only we—Amelia held up her hand and cleared her throat and said I had to stop fucking around and vote one way or the other: *Yes taxes* or *No taxes*. If I couldn't do that, she said, I should do everyone a favor and leave. I said, "It's not that simple," and she said, "It is that simple," and I said, "But what's happening can't be reduced to *This is right* or *This is wrong*. In the absence of absolutes, we have a kind of... Can we open a window? It's so hot in here. Let's just think, because people of goodwill can disagree about the remedy while agreeing on the disease. And we do, don't we? We agree on the disease. We can name it. The disease is sprawling and incomprehensible in its totality, and it spreads like cancer...like Los Angeles...and so having identified that, we can heal and establish binding laws while retaining flexibility, because sometimes we're one thing and sometimes we're another because in this post-binary.... It's really so hot. Can anyone think clearly? Is the window stuck? Are all the windows stuck? Let's get some altitude. Let's think clearly because otherwise we're going to crash into something, the ground or the sky...or...." Amelia rose from her seat and wrapped me in a blanket that burned to the touch. Then she took me to my room, where I fell into a fiery, three-day fever, which lifted only when everyone had packed up and left.

"I think I can do it," I told Mackenzie.

"Okay," she said, looking neither convinced nor unconvinced. "Talk to Bryan on your way out to sign papers and get a schedule and parking permit."

On the train home I looked at thousands of buildings made pink by the chemical sunset, and when I got back I found Amelia standing by my foldout ironing board, tracing the fabric's pattern with her finger, rubbing the burn hole.

"Love this thing," she said. Although she'd been raised in the Bronx, she had no accent, the result of five years in Portland's fixed-gear bicycle community. ("You don't feel it while it's happening, but after a while you sound like you're from nowhere.")

"How did you get in?" I untucked my shirt and removed the wingtips I'd borrowed from Saul and dug my toes into the carpet.

"The woman across the hall."

"She's not supposed to have a key." I put on music, Bach's cello suites, and as the room's lighting softened, Amelia seemed almost to sparkle, as if she were wearing glitter or tinsel. Had we really had sex? Possible things became impossible, and the tales that lasted longest and spread furthest—about the origin of the world, about falling from grace and falling from walls and falling in love, about being our brother's keeper and sinners in the hands of an angry god and proud tigers and deceitful snakes, about the end of the world—were sublime and absurd and provisional.

"I was thinking," said Amelia, who'd joined Dion and others to form Pine Ridge 2 in an old warehouse in Eugene, "that by now you'd be settling into a regular life and starting to freak out."

"Yeah?" I said. I felt hungry for more of the dried fruit Jennifer had served the night before, mangoes and plums and juju berries.

"Food's a good idea," she said, emitting points of light and walking to the kitchen area. "Do you want to know why you couldn't commit to one side or the other at Pine Ridge?"

I watched her lift a bag of groceries to the counter. "Yes."

"It wasn't because you alone saw the advantages of each position and thought they could be spliced together to form a more perfect union, and it wasn't because you had an unconscious desire to force Pine Ridge into a civil war that would tear the place apart, and it wasn't because you were having a panic attack that elevated and exaggerated the dangers of voting for one side over the other—although it looked to the rest of us like that was what was happening, that you were having a panic attack—and it wasn't because you thought the group could be pacified by liberal and evenhanded praise, a pacification that might then have sent the clouds of taxation and everything else scudding out of the sky overhead, leaving clear cobalt blue in their wake."

"Why are you talking like this?" Having grown accustomed to the points of light, I noticed the length of Amelia's hair. She'd had a pixie cut a few weeks earlier, but now it reached down to her sternum.

"I'm trying to put this in a way you'll understand, because although you spend a lot of time in your head—too much, even by the standards of lonely, confused people whose recognition of certain aspects of human nature doesn't guarantee them the only feeling that makes all of this worth it, and by all of this I, like you, mean Life—you need things to be spelled out. Not because the heat of Los Angeles is relentless and oppressive and makes clear thought difficult. And not because your brother, to whom you were once close, took nothing away from his experiences as a Cornerboy but different masturbation techniques. And not because you saw in Paul and Dion opposite aspects of yourself, suggesting that the schism you'd always located on the outside was in fact within you. And not because you identify with mystics and would be one yourself if you knew how to go about it and which variety most suits you."

"You keep saying what isn't," I said.

Amelia unpacked the groceries and lined them up on the cutting board: Chilean sea bass, sea salt, white wine vinegar, limes, a bottle of gin. "Where's your sauté pan?" she asked, opening cupboard doors and squinting into their recesses. Then, turning back to me: "Or maybe you're not hungry. Maybe we should just have a drink."

I sat on a barstool, and the more I looked, the less Amelia looked like Amelia. I said, "Mrs. Molino—"

"Mrs. Molino is my mother. Call me Odette."

I didn't want dried fruit anymore since neither Jennifer nor Amelia nor Mrs. Molino nor Odette was offering it and life was just a stay of execution. I considered the age disparity between us, the power dynamic. I considered the woman's titillations and flip cattiness. She handed me a clear fizzing beverage with a mashed lemon wedge floating along its rim.

"Maybe I won't call you anything," I said.

"That would be brave."

The cello suites raced along slowly in the background, like a fast-moving stretch of the Nile that appears still. The light pollution in Los Angeles made stars invisible. One had to take on faith what one knew to be there.

"In fairy tales," I said, "the hero will be trapped or imprisoned in the wrong body, like the Frog Prince or the Beast, and he has to find true love to be freed."

"You want to find true love." The woman swallowed her gin and tonic and had the tired, cynical expression of someone recently divorced.

"This isn't a fairy tale."

"No?"

"It's another kind of tale. I want a bigger love than true love."

"Is there one?"

"When I moved into this place I saw a couple of homeless men arguing outside. One would say one thing and the other would say something else, and out of that dissonance came a kind of concord. I was standing through that door with the Hungarian, and water was pummeling the bathtub, just pounding it, and for so long I had thought that Los Angeles was empty because it looked empty, and that Pine Ridge was full because it looked full. Really, though, their differences don't matter."

The woman finished her drink and took mine from me, set them side by side like display mates next to the sink. "They don't?"

"No more than Canada matters." The alcohol warmed me up from the inside until there seemed to be equilibrium between the air and my skin, a perfect continuum of heat. "And I started to think about the Frog Prince and the Beast, which made me think about strange things, Humpty Dumpty and tigers and street kids and Hollywood actors and businesspeople, and how they're all beyond moral expectations. No one would blame them for living strictly according to their nature, which only coincidentally has to do with good and evil. And how despite that, they seek out goodness, and how *that's* what matters. See? By not existing, God can be forgiven!" I would be paid very little for my work on vertically integrated social media, and this would free me up to find the bigger love. "It's like, it's like—pick a country, any country."

The woman turned in profile and resembled someone etched on the front or back of a coin. Staring at what hung on the wall over a cat's scratching post, a sheathed cross sword, she said, "France."

"Okay," I said. "What do you know about it? What are the first things that pop into your head?"

"Baguettes, berets, striped shirts."

"Good! What else?"

"Wine, Impressionism, existentialism."

I grew excited. "What else?"

"Accordion music, mimes, infidelity, beauty, cinema, envy—"

"Yes! And those things are everywhere, even accordion music. You're only outside looking in if you buy into the fiction of one side defined in terms of another, of north and south. At Pine Ridge and for so many years before Pine Ridge, I bought it. Isn't that funny?"

Without moving her lips, the woman said, "Let's go to bed." I reached out for her cold hands and met no resistance. Outside, people looked up at the starless night sky to count what was missing.

ACKNOWLEDGMENTS

I'd like to thank the excellent readers and editors who helped shape and house these stories early on: David Daley, Bret Anthony Johnston, Beth Staples, Laura Cogan, Fred Tangeman, G.C. Waldrep, Lee Klein, D. Laserbeam, Sudip Bose, David Gessner, Steve Erickson, and Lisa Locascio. My deepest gratitude goes out to everyone at Dzanc for their support, in particular Guy Intoci and Michelle Dotter for their editorial brilliance and Michael Seidlinger for his promotional acumen. I owe you all everything.

The following stories have been published previously:

"A Moral Tale" (*ZYZZYVA*), "Nu" (*Ecotone*), "The Stranger" (*West Branch*), "Haley" (*Joyland*), "Arising" (*The American Scholar*), "Concord" (*FiveChapters*), "Humphrey Dempsey" (*FiveChapters*), "Stargazing" (*Eyeshot*), "Jane Says" (*Freeze Frame Fiction*), "BANG" (*Black Clock*).

ABOUT THE AUTHOR

Josh Emmons is the author of two novels, *Prescription for a Superior Existence* and *The Loss of Leon Meed*. A regular contributor to *The New York Times, People,* and *The Los Angeles Review of Books,* he teaches at UC Riverside and lives with his daughter in Los Angeles, CA. Visit him on the web at joshemmons.com.